Lunch with the Alien
and Other Short, Short Stories

Lunch with the Alien
and Other Short, Short Stories

By Greg Roensch

Lunch with the Alien and Other Short, Short Stories

By Greg Roensch

Published by Greg Roensch.

ISBN 978-0-9986230-2-3

Cover art: Aimee Bruckner Design
Interior design: Dan Davis

www.gregroensch.com

For Mom

The lyf so short, the craft so longe to lerne.

– Geoffrey Chaucer, *Parlement of Foules*

Contents

Orientation

With a slate of meetings on her mind, Alice Loverly, the long-time Vice President of Human Resources, hurried into the breakroom for another dose of caffeine. What she saw froze Alice in her tracks and erased all thoughts about meetings, coffee, or anything else. Though she couldn't put her feelings into words, Alice sensed an immediate attraction to the long-fingered alien sitting at the table by the vending machines.

Crossing the room to introduce herself, Alice fought off an urge to run her fingers through the coal-black coif of wild, disheveled hair that gave the alien the look of a 1980s popstar – like one of the guys in Wham! or Duran Duran. Instead, she slid her hands over her hips to smooth out the wrinkles in her red-and-white plaid skirt. What's come over me? Alice wondered. I'm the Vice President of Human Resources for Christ-sakes.

"Welcome," said Alice. "You must be here for our lunchtime orientation."

When the creature didn't respond, Alice placed her right hand on its sinewy shoulder, her gaze lingering on those wondrous waves of dark, tousled hair.

"Don't be afraid," Alice said. "Everyone's nervous on the first day."

Alice patted the alien's shoulder reassuringly and watched in silence as its fingers twitched on the table. It reminded Alice of how Fritz, her seven-year-old cocker spaniel, shook his leg involuntary when she scratched his belly just right.

"You're in good hands now," cooed the head of Human Resources.

The alien tilted its head toward Alice. Though it didn't speak, there was something in the creature's look that let Alice know her words were not only understood but appreciated.

Without warning, the alien reached up and flopped its scaly hand on top of Alice's. Though surprised, the VP of HR gripped the hand in hers and coaxed the alien to its feet. Now standing face-to-face with the creature, Alice saw a dab of blue saliva on its chin.

"There, that's better," Alice said, wiping away the blue drool and wondering if saliva-soiled napkins should go in the trash, recycling, or compost bin.

Leading the alien out of the breakroom and down the hallway, Alice made a mental note of anyone who stared or ran in the opposite direction. Looks like we need to ramp up diversity training again, she thought.

"Don't mind them," Alice whispered. "They'll warm up to you in a few days."

Alice beamed with a sense of corporate pride when pointing out the company's state-of-the-art facilities – the recently refurbished cafeteria, the fully equipped gym, and the lush central lawn where employees flung frisbees at lunch.

"We'd better hurry," said Alice, checking her watch. "I have a meeting, and I don't want you to be late for orientation."

The alien voiced its displeasure by emitting a loud gurgle.

"There, there," Alice replied. "We'll finish the tour later."

Back in the hallway, when Alice stopped at the water faucet, the alien began to wander off toward the elevators.

"Come back over here, you sneaky devil," Alice called. "We're going this way."

As she pointed back toward the breakroom, Alice saw one of her favorite co-workers duck behind a cubicle wall in the Accounting department.

"Hey, Max," she said. "I want to introduce you to …"

Before the perky VP of HR could finish her sentence, the well-coifed alien sprung with surprising agility onto a nearby desk and headed straight for Max Marsupolis. A thick strand of blue saliva streamed from both corners of the creature's mouth, a clear sign to anyone familiar with the species that the alien, its thin brown lips stretched open to reveal two rows of piranha-sharp teeth, was on the hunt for its next meal.

Always on the Run

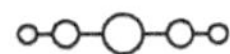

Slim sped down the highway with one hand wrapped around the steering wheel and the other gripping his Colt .45. After careening through a long, sloping, tree-lined turn, he hit the accelerator on the last straightaway before entering city limits.

"Yee-haa, baby-doll," he hollered and shot a nervous smile toward his pregnant girlfriend sprawled in the back seat. "Hang in there, Runa. We're almost there."

"Oh baby," the woman said. "I'm fixin' to pop any minute."

"We're almost there," Slim repeated, stomping down harder on the gas pedal. "You and me, Runa. You and me, we aren't long for this world."

"You're crazy, honey," said Runa. "That's why I love you so much."

They hadn't been back to the city for nearly a year, not since their getaway from the bank heist caused the fiery crash that left two cops dead on the scene.

"Slow down, Slim," said Runa. "This isn't the time to get pulled over."

Slim eased up on the accelerator. "Sorry, honey, but it's not every day a guy's gonna have a baby."

Runa grit her teeth through the pain. "You're not the one having the baby, darling."

"I know, honey-pie. I'm just excited, that's all."

Slim slowed to the speed limit and eyeballed his gun on the seat. We'd been safe in the cabin for so many months, he thought, but with our wanted posters plastered all over the city for nearly a year now, no one's gonna forget this face. Slim glanced at his heavily tattooed mug in the mirror and lit an unfiltered Camel.

"Slim, don't," Runa said. "The baby."

"What about the baby?" Slim asked, taking a long drag.

"Smoking's bad for the baby, even now, honey." Runa rubbed her belly and held her breath, as if that would protect her unborn child from the toxic cloud forming in the car.

"Alright." Slim flicked the barely smoked cigarette out the window and watched in the sideview mirror as sparks danced on the asphalt.

Runa moaned.

"God, baby-doll," Slim said. "I hate seeing you in pain. What can I do for you?"

"Just get me to the hospital in one piece," Runa answered. "That's all I want."

"We'll be there soon."

Runa wailed when they hit the speed bump in the hospital driveway. After screeching to a stop in the no-parking zone by the main entrance, Slim grabbed his pistol, leapt from the front seat, and opened the back door. As he helped Runa to her feet, Slim spotted the security guard coming their way.

"That's far enough," Slim shouted, pointing the gun at the guard. "We have some business to attend to here."

"Take it easy, mister," the guard responded. "You won't get any trouble from me."

By then Runa was bent over and holding her belly. "Wheelchair," she shouted and groaned some more.

Slim hesitated, wondering if letting the guard fetch a wheelchair was such a good idea.

"Wheelchair," Runa yelled even louder.

"Okay," Slim shouted at the guard. "You heard the lady."

"I'm moving," the man said as he hustled toward the hospital entrance. "Just quit pointing that gun at me, and I'll make sure she's next in line to see a doctor."

"Jesus, honey. It hurts. It really hurts."

"He'll be back soon, baby-doll. Hang in there."

While waiting for the guard to return, Slim bounced on the balls of his feet, a nervous habit he'd had since childhood. He got even more animated when he saw the guard coming back.

"Hurry up, man," he said. "My Runa's about to burst."

The guard was sweating hard and breathing heavily. "Alright ma'am, let's get you inside."

"Thank God," Runa replied before shrieking so loud it scattered a group of crows sitting on a nearby telephone line.

Slim followed as the guard wheeled Runa up the ramp, through the lobby, and down a long, brightly lit corridor, her moans echoing off the walls of the empty hospital and drowning out the squeal of the wheelchair's rubber tires.

The security guard stopped at the elevator bank and told Slim to push the button.

"Oh God," Runa moaned. "Oh God."

Slim stared at the illuminated panel that tracked the elevators. The moving lights reminded him of the arcade where he and Runa first met. "Number three's on its way," he called out. "We're almost there, Runa baby. We're almost there."

He ran to the elevator door and bounced some more on the balls of his feet.

"Come on, number three," he urged.

Runa let out another agonized scream like the baby would drop right there on the floor.

"Get your ass over here," said Slim, motioning to the guard.

The man held his ground. "It's best not to move her until absolutely necessary," he said. "I'll bring her over when the door opens."

The ping of the elevator signaled its arrival.

"Here we go, baby-doll," Slim said. "I love you."

"I love you, too," Runa replied through clenched teeth.

Slim was staring deeply into Runa's emerald-green eyes when the door slid open and four uniformed cops rushed the gunman, pinned him to the floor, and got in a few sharp gut punches for good measure.

"Slim!" Runa screamed, as the security guard rolled her into the elevator.

"No need to worry about Slim," said the guard. "Those boys will take good care of him."

"I told you, baby-doll, I told you," Slim shouted as the officers cuffed him.

"Told me what?" Runa yelled.

"You and me, honey. You and me, we aren't long for this world."

Still or Sparkling

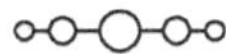

The still water bottles were happiest when the sparkling stayed on the opposite side of the shelf. In truth, both sides preferred to keep any interaction to a minimum.

The way the still water bottles saw it, their fizzy counterparts were carbonated showoffs who only came around for special occasions, like holidays or birthdays or when Aldo and Janet threw swank parties for people from the firm. Whenever the sparkling turned up, the still bottles showed their disdain by huddling together at the back of the fridge, their glass tinkling against one another when the door opened and closed.

Last Sunday was the perfect example of everything the still bottles loathed about the sparkling. It was the night before the memorial service for grandma Mavis, a two-pack-a-day smoker who died in a freak hailstorm. As the still water bottles stood front and center ready for the next day's deployment, Janet returned from a last-minute trip to the store with two cases of sparkling water.

Arrogance personified is how the still bottles described it when the sparkling took their place at the front, their fresh bubbles rushing up their necks like neon signs flashing "drink me, drink me" to anyone who opened the refrigerator door. Relegated to a dark corner far back on the shelf, where a leaf of withered kale kept company with an expired box of Arm & Hammer baking soda, the still bottles checked their anger out of respect for grandma Mavis. But deep down their resentment festered.

"Who do they think they are?" one of the still bottles asked on the day after the memorial. "It's not like they even knew the woman."

"Gassy blowhards," another old-timer muttered. "Their fizz won't last forever. And they know it."

As for the sparkling bottles, theirs had traditionally been an attitude of hushed superiority. Typically placed in the best position in the fridge, they mostly kept to themselves – as if conversing with the still bottles was beneath their station. They were elite, or so they felt. And it was with a sense of casual disregard that they thumbed their noses, so to speak, at the still water.

That said, if you asked around, you'd find that many sparkling bottles had a grudging appreciation for their hardworking colleagues.

"They're the real workhorses around here," a sparkling bottle admitted during a chat with some of his bubbly buddies.

"You're right about that," another replied.

"If you think about it long enough," a third sparkling bottle said, "you realize that we're not so different from one another."

"You know what they say?" added the sparkling who started the conversation. "There but for the grace of God, go I."

The sparkling bottles stopped talking when Chad, Aldo and Janet's pimply faced sixteen-year-old high-school sophomore, opened the refrigerator and began loading the shelves with bottles of an all-new CBD-infused, lemon-lime-flavored drink. The yellow-green concoction, looking like something you might see in a mad scientist's laboratory, was labelled with an image of a bulging-eyed, razor-fanged creature that looked like it could eat glass for breakfast, lunch, and dinner.

Chad shoved the new bottles into the fridge without any regard for the orderly placement of the others. And, after a harrowing period of noisy jostling, the still and sparkling bottles were all clustered together at the back of the shelf.

"Well, this is awkward," one of the sparkling bottles said when the door slammed shut and the light went out.

From the moment of their arrival, the monster bottles let it be known that there was a new lemon-lime-flavored sheriff in town. They glowered with their protruding eyes, growled in unintelligible guttural tones, and bared their fangs like ravenous beasts. They even knocked against the still and sparkling bottles on purpose, seemingly without any fear whatsoever of the damage they might do to themselves or anyone else. Neither the still nor sparkling bottles knew what to make of these intruders. No one in the fridge did. Not the fat-free yogurt. Not the skim milk. Not the leftover Brie in the vacuum-sealed Tupperware. Even the sliced cucumbers were agitated.

Before this chaotic new order could take hold for good, the still and sparkling bottles met in secret to discuss ways of getting rid of the monster bottles.

"Here's what we'll do," the leader of the still bottles whispered. "Tonight, when they're fast asleep, we'll nudge those crazy-eyed demons even further toward the front of the shelf. Anyone opening the fridge for a drink will grab those suckers first." She stopped to make sure the monsters weren't listening. "Once they're gone, we can get things back to normal around here."

"They won't know what hit them," a sparkling bottle exclaimed.

As it turned out, the CBD-infused monsters slept so soundly they didn't notice when they were being bumped forward. And it only took two days for the refrigerator to return to what it was like before the vile creatures arrived on the scene.

"You guys are alright," a young sparkling bottle said to a nearby still.

"You're not so bad yourself," the still replied and cozied up to her new fizzy friend.

As the still and sparkling bottles were celebrating victory, Chad was wrapping up his Saturday morning chores. He'd mowed the lawn, swept the garage, and taken out the trash. All that remained was rolling the recycling to the curb. While wheeling the blue bin down the driveway, the teen was surprised at how heavy it was, and, when he flipped open the lid, he was shocked to see one empty bottle after another of the CBD-infused monster drink. "Looks like I need to go to the store again," Chad grumbled as he made a mental note to restock the fridge with another case of his new favorite lemon-lime-flavored beverage.

Romance, Shromance

"Romance, shromance," said Ida Wingate as she tossed the dozen long-stemmed roses into the dumpster behind the pet store. She lingered for a few seconds, taking a last teary-eyed look at the bouquet before turning and walking down the alley. Who needs him anyway? Ida thought as she shuffled toward the bus stop.

Ida plopped down on the bench with a heavy sigh and eyed the scrolling bus tracker. "Next bus in 25 minutes," rolled by on the screen, right above a poster featuring the new mayor with a tagline that read, "Never wait more than 10 minutes. I guarantee it!"

"Liars," spat Ida. "They're all a bunch of liars."

A man in a wheelchair rolled into the sheltered bus stop and glanced sideways at Ida.

"Don't worry about me," she said, dabbing at her eyes with a tissue.

"Well, I don't mean to be nosy," the man said, "but …"

"Then don't be," Ida said before the man could finish his sentence.

"Excuse me?"

"Don't be nosy," Ida said. "It's none of your business."

"Yes, ma'am," the man replied while maneuvering his wheelchair into the corner. "Far be it from me to pry." He looked up at the bus tracker, which now read, "Next bus in 28 minutes."

"Damn!" he cursed.

Ida craned her neck to read the sign. "Unbelievable," she sighed and motioned toward the poster of the mayor. "They're all a bunch of liars."

"And crooks," the man added. "Don't forget about crooks."

"Liars and crooks," Ida replied, a quivering smile forming on her lips.

The man burst out with a deep, hearty laugh that had him rocking back and forth and slapping the arms of his wheelchair. It was one of those contagious belly laughs that makes you want to laugh along with it. Ida felt herself giving into laughter.

"Liars and crooks," bellowed the man. "Ain't that the truth." He nudged his chair toward Ida.

"I'm sorry about snapping at you earlier," said Ida. "I've had a bad day, that's all."

"No need to apologize," said the man, flashing a big, friendly smile. "My name's Henry," he said. "Henry T. Goodfellow."

"Get out of here," Ida replied. "That's not your real name."

"God's honest truth," answered the man. "My mother had tons of trouble when it came to men. By the time I was born, my father was long gone, and my mother was so fed up she wouldn't even give me his name. That's how 'Henry T. Goodfellow' came to be on my birth certificate. I guess she hoped it would provide me with a sense of direction."

"What an incredible story," said Ida, turning her head so the man wouldn't notice the tears rolling down her cheeks.

"Yes, indeed. And I have my mother to thank for it. God rest her soul."

"Your mother sounds like a good woman," said Ida, wiping her face.

"A good woman who gave birth to a Goodfellow," said Henry T. Goodfellow without missing a beat. And with that they both laughed again.

When it got quiet, Henry glanced up at the bus tracker. It read: "Next bus in 30 minutes."

"Half an hour," he exclaimed and chuckled. "Can you believe it?"

"We might as well spend the night," said Ida, blushing.

Henry smiled. "I have an idea."

"Yes?"

"I mean if you're not doing anything."

"Yes?" Ida said again.

"How'd you like to join me for a drink across the street."

Ida glanced at the little bar on the corner. The malfunctioning neon sign over the door read "Chance Encounters," with every other letter flickering on and off. Beyond the bar, down the alley where she'd been earlier, Ida saw a feral cat prowling around the dumpster with her discarded roses.

"Alright, Henry T. Goodfellow," said Ida, gazing now into the man's kind, smiling eyes. "You're on, but on one condition."

"What's that?"

"The drinks are on me."

"It's a deal," Henry replied. And with that he unclamped the wheel locks on his chair and began rolling across the street. Ida fell into step behind the chair, grabbed the handles, and smiled while guiding the kind man with the big belly laugh toward the cozy confines of the neighborhood bar.

"Romance, shromance," Ida said to herself. "Romance, shromance."

Going to California

I finished my whiskey when the horn blared from the parking lot.

"Come on, boys," I called to the two greyhounds at the base of my stool. "We have a bus to catch."

I slapped a dollar tip on the counter and walked toward the door. The dogs, a pair of recent rescues I named "Elmer" and "Fudd," came running for the bone-shaped treats in my hand.

"Eat up, fellas. It's a long way to Frisco."

Crossing the lot toward the idling bus, I tipped my cap in the direction of the woman who'd reluctantly sold me a one-way ticket for me and my dogs.

"There's nothing I can do about it," she'd said at first.

The ticket agent's nametag read "Deborah Hairtonic." "Tonight's bus is full."

"You might be interested to know," I said in an attempt to soften up Miss Hairtonic, "my service dogs are two of the winningest greyhounds in the history of Derby Days racetrack just outside of Tallahassee."

"I don't care if they're the second coming of Lassie and Rin Tin Tin," the woman snapped. "There's no room on the bus. The best I can do is get you on tomorrow's early bird that leaves at 5:15 AM."

Something in my gut told me the ticket agent wasn't trying her hardest to find us a seat, so I gave it one more shot. "Look," I told her, "these dogs are incredibly well-behaved."

She wasn't swayed when I showed her how Elmer and Fudd sat up, lay down, rolled over, and shook my hand – all at a few simple commands. It was only when I slipped her two fives and a ten that Miss Hairtonic finally changed her tune.

"Well, looky right here," she said, crumpling the bills in her fist and motioning toward the seating chart like she'd missed something earlier. "We do have a pair of seats after all, but they're all the way in the back by the *turlet*." She pinched her nose with her thumb and forefinger to make sure I understood her meaning.

"That'll do just fine." I glanced down at the dogs. "We aren't particular, are we, boys?"

Elmer, always eager to please, gazed up with a wide-eyed look that said, "Whatever you say, boss," while Fudd, ever the reserved one, kept his head low. He wasn't interested in much of anything other than eating and sleeping.

"Just make sure those dogs of yours take care of their business before getting on the bus." Those were Miss Hairtonic's last words before she slid the ticket window shut and flipped over the "CLOSED" sign.

"You don't have to worry about that," I hollered through the glass as the dogs sauntered over to a nearby clump of Mexican Firebush and relieved themselves like ... well, I was going to say like racehorses, but the fact of the matter is that these dogs were prodigious urinators in their own right. So, I'll just go ahead and say they pissed like the pedigreed canines they were bred to be.

It didn't take long for my greyhounds to get comfortable in our seats by the *turlet*. Elmer lay on the seat next to me, resting his chin on my thigh, while Fudd curled up into a ball on the floor, his tail thumping out a beat on the carpet. As our driver walked down the aisle for a final passenger count, I heard a siren and watched as a police car, its red and blue lights flashing, screeched to a halt in front of the bus station.

"Let's get this show on the road," I wanted to tell the driver when he stopped his headcount to stare out at the commotion.

By now, everyone on the bus was watching as a state trooper hustled out of his car and knocked hard on the ticket window to get Miss Hairtonic's attention. I'll admit my heartbeat was on hyperdrive, because I knew for a fact that the lawman was looking for me. You see, when I mentioned earlier that Elmer and Fudd were rescue dogs, the reality is that I stole these two pooches from the racing kennel where I'd worked as a handyman for the past four months.

Starved at times. Overfed at others. And living in unsanitary and cramped conditions. These dogs suffered from a lifetime of horrendous treatment. Hell, I would have freed all 243 dogs in the kennel if I could, but something about Elmer and Fudd tugged extra hard at my heartstrings.

When the driver finally put the bus in gear, I glanced over at the ticket window just in time to catch Miss Hairtonic shake her head as if to say, "Nope, I haven't seen any dogs around here tonight." Based on her body language, I could tell Miss Hairtonic wasn't a fan of the local authorities. And when she turned her head to shoot me a subtle wink, I breathed a deep sigh of relief, knowing then that my twenty dollars had been money well spent.

Dark Walk

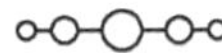

It was one of those nights when I stopped by the bar
with every intention of having one drink – and one
drink only. Don't ask me how things devolved into shot
after shot until closing time.

Standing beneath the neon hiss of the "COCKTAILS"
sign, I lit a cigarette and thought about calling a cab.
But the night was warm – and I could use the fresh air –
so I set out for home on foot. And I didn't come across
anyone until I was halfway through the tunnel by the
tracks. That's when I heard the slow, shuffling footsteps.

The man came out from the darkness. Tall and
lumbering, he wore tattered clothes and walked as if
he'd suffered through a botched surgical procedure.

From a distance, his face looked like it was inked with tattoos, but when he came closer, I saw it was a patchwork of hideous scars.

Steeling myself to pass the scar-faced man, I was forced to stop when he veered into my path.

"I, monster," he said in a hoarse voice.

"Excuse me?" I asked.

"I, monster," he repeated.

"Whatever, buddy." I attempted to sidestep the stranger, but he moved with surprising quickness.

"You stay."

He punctuated his command with a shove to my chest.

"Hey," I said. I was sobering up now.

The man leaned closer, a foul stench coming from his mouth.

"I, monster," he said again.

"You, crazy," I replied.

When I tried again to walk away, he grabbed my coat with both hands.

"What are you doing?" I struggled in vain to shake loose.

"You stay!" he bellowed.

Before I knew what was happening, the stranger released my coat and wrapped his fingers around my throat.

"I, monster," he shouted one last time. "I, hungry."

Shipwreck

I saved three albums from the shipwreck and played them on the desert island until every note – and every crack, pop, and warble – was etched into my brain. I listened to them so much I heard them in my sleep. I even heard them after the old turntable gave out. Now, seven years after my rescue, I'm still haunted by those albums. I refuse to play them – or even speak their names.

The Fishbowl

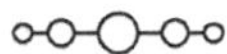

I lived above a bar with a dusty golden Buddha in the
corner. It was a surprisingly quiet place, except for
the occasional fistfight. That all changed on the night
of the armed robbery, when a bullet ricocheted off the
Buddha, came up through the floor of my apartment,
deflected off the coffee table, and landed in the fishbowl
next to my old television. The fish was fine, but I knew
then that it was time to move.

An Adventure in Art Appreciation

Mel waved his arm like a commando leading a raid on an enemy bunker. "Hurry up," he called to his wife. "This place closes in an hour."

"I'm right behind you," Emily replied, pausing to catch her breath at the base of the long marble staircase before beginning her ascent to the museum's second floor.

Mel knew this was going to be a long day when Emily had made reservations for a Henry VIII-themed lunch, an event that was too expensive and took far too long.

"Let's go," Mel shouted when Emily reached the top stair. He was on the move again, nearly barreling into a woman posing for a selfie in front of a falcon-headed sphinx.

"Sorry," Mel said and rushed onward.

"Are you sure this is the right way?" Emily asked.

"Yes, I'm sure," Mel said over his shoulder. He'd studied the museum floorplan at breakfast. After ancient Mesopotamia, we'll pass through the Egyptian collection, he thought. It'll be the Greeks next, then the special exhibit. "Come on," he said, gesturing with another commando wave.

"I'm coming."

For three weeks, Mel had been on a quest to have his picture taken with as many great European artworks as possible, checking them off one by one like he was collecting baseball cards. From city to city, museum to museum, exhibit to exhibit, Emily had snapped shots of Mel with the masters. Mel and Van Gogh. Mel and Picasso. Mel and da Vinci. The list went on. So, she wasn't surprised by her husband's outburst on the train the previous night.

"How'd we miss that?" Mel exclaimed as they sped through a small station.

"Miss what?" Emily stirred from a brief nap.

"*The Scream*," Mel said. "It's at the British Museum."

"But tomorrow's the last day of our vacation and we already have lunch reservations," Emily reminded him. "We won't have time."

"We can make the time if we leave the lunch early."

For Emily, spending their last afternoon being served by waiters in Tudor costumes had seemed like a fun and relaxing way to wrap up their European vacation. Once Mel saw the poster for *The Scream*, however, Emily knew her husband wouldn't rest until he had his picture taken with one of the world's most famous paintings.

Mel charged through Mesopotamia, past gold and silver containers, earrings and beaded necklaces, chisels and sewing needles, and a trove of other artifacts. He hesitated briefly to look at the mummified remains of a Sumerian woman, her head encircled by an ornate gold band, before pushing ahead into the Egyptian rooms.

"Excuse me." Mel spread his hands to cut through the crowd of tourists gathered around the mummies.

"Keep coming," he shouted to Emily. "We're almost there."

If Emily heard him, she didn't respond. And when Mel looked back, he couldn't see her.

"Go through the Greek rooms," he yelled. "I'll meet you at the painting."

Mel picked up his pace again, darting through a series of rooms filled with Grecian urns, vases, and statues. He was sweating by the time he spotted the door marked "Special Exhibit."

"I found it," Mel said in a hushed voice at first and then again more loudly as he strode through the sliding door. "I found it!"

Standing in the middle of a large gallery with his hands on his hips, Mel was ready to have his picture taken with the iconic masterpiece. Instead, he found himself turning from one wall to another in an empty room. Where's everyone? he wondered. Where's *The Scream*? He was about to go into the adjoining gallery when the sliding door opened behind him. Expecting his wife, Mel was surprised to see a burly guard coming his way.

"I'm sorry, sir," the guard said, his meaty hands balled into fists. "I'm afraid we've had a number of complaints."

Before Mel could respond, the door opened again, and Emily rushed into the room.

"Oh my," she said. "What's the problem?"

"No problem, ma'am," the guard answered. "I was just explaining to this gentleman that we've had complaints from other visitors."

"I'm so sorry ..."

"Where is it?" Mel blurted, cutting off his wife.

"Mel!" Emily gasped, her face reddening.

"Excuse me, sir," the guard said, "you'll have to lower your voice."

"We're in the special exhibit room, aren't we?" Mel turned from one wall to the next as if *The Scream* might appear if he looked hard enough.

"Sir, I'm asking you for the last time."

"And I'm asking you for the last time," Mel shouted. "Where's *The Scream*?"

"*The Scream*?"

"Yes, *The Scream*. Where is it?"

"Well," the guard replied as two of his colleagues came into the room. "I suppose it's back in Oslo by now."

"Oslo? What are you talking about? I saw it on a poster last night. *The Scream* is here."

"You might have seen a poster," the guard explained, "but the exhibit ended last week." He motioned to the empty gallery. "We're preparing for the next show. Now, if you'll be so kind as to follow me."

Mel looked over at his wife.

"Emily, I …"

"Hold it," Emily said to the security guards as they led Mel from the gallery.

"What are you doing?"

Emily pulled a camera from her purse and snapped a picture of Mel with the three guards.

"I'll see you back at the hotel," Emily said over her shoulder as she left the gallery alone.

Retracing her steps through Greece, then Egypt, then Mesopotamia, before descending the great marble staircase and exiting into the brisk late-afternoon chill of Bloomsbury, Emily stepped with a deliberate pace, the heavy tapping of her heels on the pavement signaling to the world that her vacation was over. She was ready to go home.

Christmas Ghosts

There was only one present under the tree – one lonely gift wrapped in gold paper topped with a shiny red bow. It was about the size of a cigar box, though I knew it couldn't be that. No one was allowed to smoke in here.

*

My mind drifted back to those long-ago Christmas gatherings when the entire family descended upon our two-story, red-roofed house in the Avenues. On a clear day you could see all the way to the ocean.

Relatives came from near and far. Aunts and uncles, first and second cousins. Some even came all the way from the Philippines. We'd all take turns speaking on the telephone to those who couldn't make it.

"*Magandang umaga*," I remember someone on the other end of the line saying.

"Good morning," I replied. "Merry Christmas."

*

My grandparents, my Lolo and Lola, brought the Christmas tree out of storage every year. It was a seven-foot-tall plastic tree with bristly branches like oversized pipe cleaners. And it rotated on a metal base containing a speaker that looped tinny renditions of classic carols, though I can't remember which ones.

The manger scene barely fit under the tree. The heads of the three wisemen and the shepherds stuck up into the last row of plastic bristles, like they were lost in the clouds. There were so many gifts stacked under the tree by Christmas that you couldn't even see the swaddled baby Jesus.

*

"Merry Christmas," the nurse said and placed a tray on my table. "I'll be back to pick it up in an hour."

I rolled forward in my wheelchair and lifted the metal lid to uncover a plateful of overcooked turkey, runny mashed potatoes, and soggy vegetables.

"Merry Christmas," I whispered, but the nurse had already left the room.

*

I recalled sprinting up the front staircase of my grandparents' house and making a beeline for the appetizers. Chips and dips. Nuts and olives. Almond-encrusted cheeseballs and homemade lumpia. I'd be a millionaire, I thought, if I had a dollar for every lumpia I ate back then. I made a motion with my hand of dipping a deep-fried roll into a cup of vinegar and soy sauce. I could almost taste it.

The main course consisted of ham and turkey, mashed potatoes and gravy, string beans and grilled onions, and bread stuffing. We also had Filipino food. Not just lumpia, but pancit, adobo, and other dishes with names I could never remember.

There was a separate table just for dessert. Cookies, pies, candy-canes, and other treats. Everyone loved Lola's homemade flan.

*

After the meal, we'd cram into the living room to open presents. One year, when I was six or seven, I received a gift from an uncle who'd just returned from the Philippines. It was a wood plaque decorated with miniature swords from Mindanao.

"I already have one of these," I said and handed the plaque back.

"*Coño*," my father scolded. "Say 'thank you' to your uncle."

"Thank you," I said, but I didn't mean it.

*

"Well, haven't you been a naughty boy?" The nurse's words caught me by surprise. I didn't remember wheeling across the room or placing the gold-wrapped present in my lap.

When she reached for the package, I held it tight and refused to let go.

"Have it your way," she said, "but this is going in your report."

Thinking back again to our family gatherings in the Avenues, I tore off the wrapping paper and opened the gift – only to find out it was empty inside.

Daddy Long Legs

On his way to school, Gus found himself walking
behind Jimmy and Vinnie Mussleman as they were
talking about spiders. Three years ahead of Gus
at Christ the Redeemer, the twins were all-league
linebackers with a reputation for being neighborhood
bullies.

"I thought you were going to flush it down the toilet,"
said Jimmy.

"I did flush it," Vinnie answered, "after tearing off its
legs."

The brothers laughed in a whiny, high-pitched squeal
that was often heard on the gridiron after they made a
big play.

"Did you see those legs twitch?" Vinnie asked, which set off another round of squealing that died out when they noticed Gus.

"Hey, wart," said Jimmy, calling Gus by the name given to freshmen at Christ the Redeemer.

"Wart! Wart! Wart!" Vinnie chanted, like a war cry.

Gus slowed down to put some distance between himself and the brothers.

"Smart move, wart," Jimmy said. "Stay away or we might pull your legs off."

Vinnie made an exaggerated tweezing motion with his right hand, snapping his thumb shut against his fingers and jerking his arm away to show Gus what it would look like to have his legs ripped from his body. Gus stopped walking, hoping the brothers would leave him alone.

"Don't worry," Vinnie said, "we're late for class, or we'd stick around and have some fun."

"Wart! Wart! Wart!" the brothers grunted as they kept walking.

Gus stood still and listened as the war cries and high-pitched laughter faded into the distance. When he was sure the brothers were gone, Gus breathed a sigh of relief and continued on his way to school.

A few days later, in the cafeteria, Gus heard a familiar squeal coming from a nearby table.

"That's gross," exclaimed Cindy Riordan, a redheaded cheerleader and the prettiest girl in town, at least Gus thought so.

"You're nasty," said Suzy Belasco, another cheerleader and Cindy's best friend.

"Oh, come on," Vinnie said to the girls. "Don't tell me you have a thing for spiders?"

"Yeah," Jimmy chimed in. "You're not a couple of kinky weirdos, are you?"

"Ew," said Cindy. "That's gross."

"No, we don't have a thing for spiders," said Suzy, "but that doesn't mean it's okay to torture them."

"Exactly," Cindy added, annunciating each syllable to emphasize her disgust.

"Lighten up already." Jimmy made a motion of flicking a lighter in his left hand while waving an imaginary aerosol can in the right, like he was spraying the girls with a homemade blowtorch. "Lighten up," he said again. "Get it?"

"Good one," Vinnie snorted. "Lighten up. Like we lit up those spiders last night."

The brothers' loud squealing caused heads to turn throughout the cafeteria.

"Jerks," said Cindy, picking up her lunch tray.

Suzy rose and followed her friend to another table.

Jimmy and Vinnie continued laughing while looking around to see if anyone was watching. Whatever you do, Gus thought, keep your head down. Don't make eye contact.

"Hey, look over there," Vinnie said. "It's that dumb wart."

"Wart! Wart! Wart!"

Gus scooched to the edge of the bench and calculated the best path to the nearest exit. Thankfully, the bell rang to signal the end of lunch. As relieved as he was, Gus knew it was only a matter of time before he'd face the brothers. What can I do? he thought. They're bigger and stronger than me. And there are two of them. I don't have a chance.

When Gus fell asleep that night, he dreamed of the twins. They were older now and living in the green-and-white mansion next to the park. They were also married in the dream, and they both had two children, though it didn't take long for more kids to arrive on the scene. Kids squeezed through doors and windows. They slid down the chimney. They even wriggled through cracks in the walls and floor, all of them squealing at the top of their lungs.

With the house bursting at the seams with screaming children, Jimmy and Vinnie slipped into the garage, which was spotless, sterile, and brightly lit like a hospital operating room.

"I've been looking forward to this all day," said Vinnie, walking to a stainless-steel table and slipping his hands into tight rubber gloves.

"You're not the only one," Jimmy replied. He reached into a box on the table with a pair of tweezers, pulled out a fat, hairy, brown spider, and held it up to the buzzing florescent light before placing it on the table, which was now set for two with crystal wine glasses, bone china plates, sterling silver dinnerware, and red silk napkins. Vinnie picked up his knife and fork, sliced the plump spider into two uneven pieces, and gobbled down the larger half, its legs squirming as they slid down his throat.

"Delicious," Vinnie said.

Wolf, crab, and ant spiders. Wandering, recluse, and cellar spiders. Black widows and golden silk orb-weavers. Tarantulas and daddy long legs. The box on the table contained an endless supply of arachnids of all colors, shapes, and sizes. Jimmy and Vinnie were gorging themselves on one spider after another when a tremor shook the room.

"What was that?" Jimmy asked, his mouth full of spider legs.

"It's just an earthquake," Vinnie answered. "Finish your dinner."

A second jolt, bigger this time, was accompanied by a thunderous roar.

"That's not an earthquake!" Jimmy cried.

Before Vinnie could respond, an even louder roar came from above as the roof split in two and a long, spindly, claw-like appendage waved across the gaping hole where the ceiling had been.

"Let's get out of here!" Jimmy shouted.

An ear-splitting howl stopped the brothers in their tracks and drew their attention up to the gigantic, sagging underbelly of a huge daddy long legs. The creature thrust its massive leg downward with such violence it punched a hole in the concrete floor and shook the entire house. Deafening screams of terror came from the adjoining room, causing Jimmy and Vinnie to look over and see a second monster spider spear Vinnie's wife with one of its legs and dangle her over its gaping mouth.

"No!" Vinnie shrieked, but it was too late. His wife's blood-curdling screams were snuffed out in a flash when the spider tore off her head.

Yet another spider – this one a massive tarantula – reached out to lift two of Jimmy's boys off the ground.

"Daddy!" they wailed while trying to break free. "Daddy!"

Jimmy tried to step toward his sons, but his feet were glued to the floor, stuck in place by ankle-deep webbing. It was the same with Vinnie. Struggling in vain to free themselves, the brothers could only watch as an army of giant spiders devoured their children, one by one. By the time the feeding frenzy was over, Jimmy and Vinnie were slumped to their knees in the sticky goo and sobbing uncontrollably. Their cries of grief were soon drowned out, however, by an eardrum-rupturing squeal from above. The neighborhood bullies cast their tear-filled eyes skyward to see the monstrous, churning jaws of a gargantuan daddy long legs coming toward them.

"How did you sleep, honey?" Gus's mother asked when he came down to breakfast.

"I had a dream about spiders," Gus answered.

"Oh, my goodness," his mother replied. "That sounds scary."

"Not really," Gus said and took a sip of orange juice. "It was kind of cool."

The Secret Bunker

We fled toward the bunker when the bombs fell. Although we'd been trained to expect a strike at any time, we were surprised by the suddenness of this noiseless attack. Where was the roar of the squadron? Where were the warning calls or air-raid sirens? Before the chaos, I'd been tending to the sheep with Sheba, our beloved sheepdog. It had been a peaceful, sunny day in the pasture, with the wind whistling through the leaves and birdsong, bleating, and barking in the air.

While sprinting to the farmhouse, I counted at least six buildings obliterated, though most of the bombs were exploding in the open fields. I watched in horror as a flock of my father's prized herd took a direct hit, their woolly parts strewn across my path. It was at this point that I lost track of Sheba, her bark drowned out by the deafening barrage. I hated to leave her behind, but I knew enough to keep running, remembering father's instructions not to stop for anyone or anything during a raid.

I was the last to scamper into the bunker beneath our kitchen. Father yanked the steel door shut in time to protect us from the force of a nearby blast. As the air cleared in our underground hideout, I flashed back to a memory of my brother and sister and me chasing each other in and out of the shelter while father shored up the walls, installed the generator, and built the shelves that mother would stock with canned foods, medicine, and other supplies.

"How long will we stay down here?" I asked father when the dust settled.

"I don't know," he answered. "We'll see how it goes."

"The troops will come soon," mother said.

"Yes," father replied, "but we'll be safe if we're quiet."

"We all need to be very quiet," mother told us.

We nodded. Being the eldest, I took it upon myself to reinforce mother's message by raising my finger to my cracked lips.

"Ssshhh," I whispered to my frightened siblings.

"No talking," my sister whispered back in a quivering voice. "Like in the library."

"That's right." I gave her a gentle pat on the shoulder. "Like in the library."

We all gasped when the soldiers clomped into the kitchen above us.

Father reached for the service blaster he had from his days patrolling the front during the First War to Divide the States. Mother held a meat cleaver, pointing the large blade upwards with a wild-eyed look that told me she'd slit the throat of anyone who opened that door. Scanning my corner of the bunker, I caught sight of a rusty corkscrew, reached over to pick it up, and pressed the tip against my thumb to test its sharpness. If father and mother were prepared to fight, then I was too.

As the soldiers stomped and scuffed their dirty boots on our kitchen floor, I strained to decipher their muffled words. It was all unintelligible grunts until a voice came through louder than the rest to order the soldiers to search our home. "Leave nothing," the commander ordered, his words followed by the sound of plates smashing and glass shattering. We all flinched – and I gripped my corkscrew tighter – when a booming thud shook the floor. It was our old iron stove, I realized when the soldiers began kicking pots across the floor.

We remained deathly quiet, hoping they'd realize we had nothing of value, when my sister began to sob.

"Ssshh," I whispered. "Like the library."

Mother cupped her hand over my sister's mouth.

Had they heard us? I wondered when the soldiers stopped their racket. Have they found our secret door? Were they preparing to storm our secret bunker? Or were they simply done ransacking our kitchen?

Leave us alone, I wanted to shout. We never caused you any trouble.

We all held our breath when the commander returned, shouting again at the top of his voice, which set off another round of destruction. Mother removed her hand from my sister's mouth, warning her with a look not to make another peep.

After more clatter, the noise eventually died down again.

"They're done," father whispered.

"Thank God," mother replied.

My brother and sister and I remained quiet, with our eyes glued to the door at the top of the ladder. Please go away, I silently implored as if in prayer. Go away and never return. Indeed, the soldiers were making their way out of the kitchen when I heard a faint noise in the distance. It was barely audible at first. Were more troops on the way? I wondered. Or were the resistance fighters coming to our aid? That's it, I thought when a gunshot rang out – the resistance is coming to save us.

Another shot was followed by the commander's order to "stop wasting bullets."

The soldier who pulled the trigger must have missed, because the mysterious sound was still out there, and it was now becoming louder by the second – whatever was making that sound was coming straight for the house.

Mother was the first to recognize the noise. "No," she whispered.

Father and I looked into each other's eyes, realizing that we also knew the familiar sound of our sheepdog barking as it bound toward the farmhouse. And it was only a matter of seconds before the soldiers were stomping back into the kitchen as Sheba clawed at the flooring above our heads.

"Go away," mother shouted, her voice drowned out by the horrific clang of rifle butts banging against the trapdoor. "Go away, you stupid dog."

Sheba barked louder when the soldiers began to break through the door. Placing a boot on the first rung of the ladder, father aimed his pistol upwards and prepared to climb. Mother clenched her blade, ready to follow. And I clutched the rusty old corkscrew in my trembling fist while both of my siblings howled in terror. No one shushed them anymore.

One of These Days

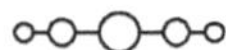

The one-eyed cat hissed and scrambled out the screen door.

Salty Jack, the old shopkeeper, put down the obsidian paperweight he was about to hurl at the scrawny feline.

"Mangy old fleabag," he spat, his spittle scattering the gang of fruit flies that had descended on the week-old cherry pie on the counter.

"One of these days," he said, "I'm gonna get that cat."

The old man reached for his Bowie knife and ran his arthritic thumb over the tip of the blade.

"Mangy old fleabag," he muttered again.

When the screen door creaked, Jack looked up to see the one-eyed cat slink back into the store. If he didn't know better, the old man would have thought the old puss was grinning.

"One of these days," he repeated, "I'm gonna wring your scraggly neck."

Instead of unleashing her usual asthmatic hiss, the cat reared back and howled. And before the dumbfounded shopkeeper could think about grabbing his obsidian paperweight, Bowie knife, or anything else, the one-eyed cat shot across the room and leapt for the old man's throat, burying her claws deep into his face and sinking her fangs into his leathery neck.

The cat held on even as Salty Jack fell backwards off his stool and cracked his skull on the hardwood floor, his screams changing quickly into a muted gurgling noise.

Across the street, an old woman shut the door of her battered van and limped toward the shop. For decades, she'd roamed the backroads, travelling from town to town selling rare tonics and charms. Just last week, she'd been kicked out of Salty Jack's, the old man saying he didn't want any toothless hags scaring off his customers.

"Here, kitty, kitty," cooed the woman in the sing-song voice she used to control her familiars. The cat responded with a loud, long, satisfied purr before releasing her grip and bolting out the door, leaving behind a trail of slick, red paw prints.

Barely conscious, Salty Jack groaned.

"Remember me?" the old woman asked, emitting a raspy cackle when seeing the flash of recognition in the man's eyes.

Kneeling beside the shopkeeper, the woman opened a satchel containing a few empty Mason jars, a rubber suction hose, and other tools of her arcane craft.

"This won't take long," she whispered while inserting the hose into one of the wounds on the old man's neck and filling the first jar. "Not long at all."

Chewie

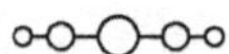

People called him Chewie because he was tall, had a shaggy beard, and roared like a Wookiee. When the cops finally caught up to us on the outskirts of Reno, Chewie scampered down the fire escape, leaving me behind to take the rap for our recent run of convenience store robberies. The real Chewie wouldn't have left Han behind, I thought as the cops cuffed me, read me my rights, and threw me into the back of the patrol car.

An Eagle

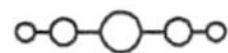

I dreamt I could fly when I lived in chains. Sometimes I'd be a robin or a swallow or any kind of bird really. I'd glide over valleys and mountains, skim lakes and rivers, and soar on warm Mediterranean breezes. One day, I dreamt I was a sparrowhawk. I wasn't in the air for long when I awoke to the sound of loud metallic clanking. And when I rose from my bunk to the shouts of the prison guards, I prayed with all my heart that I'd be an eagle in my next life.

Weekend in Tomales Bay

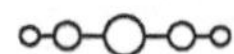

(1)

The woman paused to tighten her faux-fur-lined hood before pressing on toward the shack at the end of the pier.

"Nice boat," she remembered saying to the man when she'd taken the same walk earlier in the day after checking in to the hotel across the road. She'd surprised herself by speaking to the stranger.

"Thanks," he said. "I'm getting her ready for tonight."

"Tonight?"

"Yes, it'll be beautiful under the stars."

"Oh, I wouldn't have thought of sailing at night."

"There's going to be a full moon. Why don't you join me?"

"I might just do that," the woman replied before turning and walking back down the pier.

"I'll be waiting," the man said.

At least that's what she thought he said, but it had been hard to make out his words with the wind whipping through the tall trees near the shore and the water slapping against the pilings.

Now, with the moonlight shimmering on the bay, the woman caught the flicker of a flame in the shack window – and the glow of the boatman's cigarette. I'd heard him right, she thought. He's waiting.

(2)

"It's just a drill," the hostess said to the crowd gathered outside the restaurant.

Everyone had rushed out to see what the commotion was about. First, there'd been an ambulance, siren blaring as it roared into the parking lot next to the boat launch. Then came another emergency response vehicle, a truck hauling two jet skis that were quickly dispatched into the water and speeding across the bay.

"It's just a drill," the hostess repeated.

A helicopter flew toward the crowd, keeping low to the water before landing in the parking lot.

"It's just a …"

The hostess stopped talking when she saw the responders pull Bill Handley from the helicopter. Her hands covering her mouth, she flashed back to early that morning when she and Tom had been listening to the tide report on the radio.

"Will it be safe?" she'd asked while watching her husband get ready to take their boat out to the muddy patch of land known as "Clam Island."

"Don't worry," he'd told her and kissed her cheek. "Bill and I have been out in worse than this."

The hostess screamed when she saw the paramedics pull a second body from the helicopter – she knew then that this was not a drill.

(3)

The old man gripped the champ by the elbow and guided him away from the bar.

"Why're we leaving so early?" the retired boxer slurred.

"We have a long drive to Vegas tomorrow."

"But we just got here."

That was seven drinks ago, thought the old man as he nudged the former pugilist toward the door. "Alright, champ," he said. "Let's get you back to your room."

A booming voice echoed from the opposite end of the bar. "Well, I'll be damned if it isn't the heavyweight champion of the world."

In the fifteen years since he'd been leading the champ from one promotional event to the next, the old man had learned to steer clear of two types of people. The first was the hardcore fan, the kind of guy who'd ply the champ with drinks until closing time, asking question after question about one bout or another. The second was the wise ass with something to prove.

"Hey, champ!" shouted the guy at the end of the bar. "I'm talking to you."

"I got this," the boxer said, shaking loose from the old man's grip and turning toward the loudmouth. "I got this."

(4)

The guitar player had just downed his third shot of tequila when a woman in dangerously high heels came forward with a twenty-dollar bill in hand.

"Would you mind singing 'Happy Birthday' to my husband?" she asked. "His name's Jack."

"It'll be my pleasure," the guitar player said and tipped his cap.

Everyone in the restaurant clapped in time when the guitar player started a rollicking version of the birthday song. It was all going great until he blanked on the guy's name, singing "Happy Birthday" to "Jake" instead of "Jack."

"Jack!" the woman in dangerous heels shouted. "His name is Jack!"

Instead of correcting his mistake, the guitar player continued to sing the wrong name.

"Jake."

"Jack!"

"Jake."

"Jack!"

Back and forth, they yelled at each other until the song was over.

Long after he'd been escorted out of the restaurant by the manager, the guitar player sat in his pickup and finished off a pint of Jack Daniels he kept in the glove compartment. Jake or Jack? he thought. Jack or Jake? Who gives a rat's ass? He snickered and turned the key in the ignition.

Early the next morning, a jogger found the truck overturned in a ditch. Still buckled into his seat, the guitar player hung upside down, his purple tongue dangling from his mouth and his old guitar smashed to bits by the side of the road.

(5)

The liquor truck idled in front of the restaurant across the road from the hotel. After setting the alarm on his phone, the driver leaned his head back and pulled his baseball cap down over his eyes. It'll be another hour or so, he thought, before the manager shows up.

On the other side of the road, two maids rolled their cleaning carts toward their first room of the day.

"Housekeeping." The first maid knocked on the door.

They both looked out at the bay while waiting for an answer.

"It's different from yesterday," the second maid said.

A pair of gulls skimmed the smooth water.

"Yes," the first replied. "It's much more peaceful."

Two boats were in the yard next to the hotel. One, the "Black Pearl," was a weather-beaten rust bucket that hadn't seen the water for years. The other was a wooden skiff the hotel owner had turned into a colorful planter box.

"Housekeeping," the first maid said again, knocking once more before using her pass key.

Inside the room, the maids were surprised to see it hadn't been used. The bed was made, the towels hung in the bathroom, and the woman's suitcase remained unpacked at the foot of the bed.

"Where do you think she spent the night?" the second maid asked.

"It's none of our business," answered the first.

"I'm just curious, that's all." She looked around to make sure no other guests were listening, then whispered. "I hope she had a good time."

"It's none of our business." The first maid said again before shutting the door and pushing her cleaning cart to the next room.

(6)

On Monday morning, the police chief sat at the counter sipping coffee and thinking back to everything that happened over the weekend – the clammers drowning in the bay, the boxer in jail for smashing the loudmouth's jaw, the guitar player strangled by his seat belt, and the woman who'd last been seen walking down the pier toward the boat named "Never Too Late."

"What a weekend," the chief said to the waitress as she poured a refill. "What a weekend."

The Holding Area

You see her at the bracket sheets posted on the wall – the tall girl from Florida. It's been a year since you fought her, since she beat you with a last-second flick of a roundhouse that barely touched your helmet. The judges scored it, and that was that. She took the gold and a spot on the junior national team.

"Good luck today," you say and give her a nod.

"You, too," she replies and turns away.

You follow her with your eyes as she walks with a champion's swagger toward the other side of the holding area. Even though you haven't seen Florida since your last fight, you know from checking out her team's website that she's undefeated this year. So am

I, you remind yourself. You feel the adrenaline flowing and take a deep breath, knowing from the bracket that you're on opposite sides of the draw and won't get a rematch unless you both make it to the gold-medal round. You have to win three fights to get there, including your first match against a newcomer from Idaho.

"Good luck," you repeat under your breath, "until we meet in the finals."

Back in your team's warm-up area, you sit on the padded floor and watch as dozens of fighters are getting ready for their matches. All weight divisions. All ages. All levels. Girls. Boys. Women. Men. Kicking. Punching. Shouting. Sweating. You take a sip of water and listen to the short, powerful screams – the *keups* – of the other competitors. And the sharp slaps of their taped and padded feet on red and blue vinyl target paddles. Coach Kay says the keup gives you power. It also swats away the butterflies soaring like giant birds in the pit of your stomach.

"Match 23," a voice calls out over the PA. "Match 23. Bring your pads, your paperwork, and your coaches to the check-in table. You'll be in Ring 6."

You look down at the badge hanging from your neck to confirm – again – that you're match 94. It'll be at least two more hours until it's time to warm up. You glance over to where Idaho is kicking target paddles. Left leg roundhouse. Right leg. Motion in and out. Slide-step and kick. She has good techniques, you think, but she's running out of gas. When her coach calls out another drill, Idaho has to rest before continuing. You'd like to throw a few kicks to loosen up – and to show Idaho how you're going to run circles around her in the ring – but it's better to rest for now. Coach Kay will let you know when it's time to kick out.

When you peek over at the team from Florida, the tall girl is talking and laughing with her teammates. It looks like they're taking selfies and texting them to each other. She's so calm, you think. So confident. You lower your eyes when she looks your way and lie back against your gear bag. Relax, you tell yourself. You close your eyes and listen to Beyoncé in your earbuds.

> *"Sometimes I go off ... I go hard ...*
> *take what's mine ... I'm a star."*

Someone nearby, a coach, is calling out his fighter. "Is that all you got?" You've seen coaches like this all your life and are grateful for the way Coach Kay gets his point across without being a jerk. "Kick harder!" the coach yells. "My three-year-old daughter hits harder than that." His competitor blasts the paddle as hard as he can, the increased effort punctuated by a loud keup. But it's still not enough. "Really?" the coach shouts. "We might as well go home if that's the best you can do."

You turn up the volume and visualize an upcoming match. Not against Idaho. You already have a game plan for her. Now you're imagining a more experienced competitor, someone faster and stronger. Thinking back to the bracket sheets, you figure it might be Texas. You've seen her at many tournaments and know she's a good fighter. With your eyes still closed, you play the familiar scene in your head. You bow and shake hands. You snap into your fighting stance and wait for the referee's command to begin – "*say jak*!" From the start, you control the ring, moving smoothly from side to side and frustrating Texas with your quickness. Just before the end of the round, you read a twitch of her hip and nail her with a back kick to the solar plexus.

Opening your eyes, you see Texas jumping rope across the room. She looks like she can keep it going all day as the rope taps out a steady rhythm on the mat. She's in great shape, but you know from watching her over the years that she can be too aggressive at times, especially in big matches. You replay the last seconds from your visualization, this time starting the final sequence with a hard fake, a jolt so sudden it baits Texas into throwing her roundhouse. You see it coming and smack her in the face with a spin kick. "Keup!" You scream and pump both fists to let the judges and the whole world know you just scored with that headshot. As you're celebrating the perfect kick in your mind, you flash back to a recent sparring session at the *dojang* – the studio.

"Do you know what this is good for?" Coach Kay asked as he held both ends of his black belt.

None of the students answered.

"Come on," he said and repeated his question, "doesn't anyone know what this is good for?" Coach Kay dropped the belt and paused a few seconds before making his point with the timing of a comedian delivering a punchline.

"It's good for holding up your pants," he said and laughed.

When the giggles died down, the coach turned serious. "Always train to be the best," he instructed the class, "but remember to stay humble."

You think again about your draw. Idaho first. Then it'll probably be Texas. Then who? Anything can happen in this sport – injuries, upsets, bad luck, poor refereeing – but if you have to pick someone else to make it into the medal rounds it would be Hawaii. You've had your share of battles against her over the years, including your first tournament as five-year-old yellow belts. There wasn't any strategy back then. It was just kick, kick, kick until the referee pulled you apart.

You remember how your most recent match against Hawaii could have gone either way until Coach Kay had you switch your stance in the final round to throw her off balance.

"She's a tough fighter," Coach Kay said after the match.

"Yes, sir," you replied, wondering why he didn't congratulate you on the win.

"And, so are you!" he added and gave you a fist bump.

Work hard, you remind yourself. And stay humble.

You look over at Hawaii and see she's kicking out with her team. Not only is she a tough fighter, but she also has the loudest keup you've ever heard. Even when warming up, she screams so loud it makes everyone in the holding area look to see who's kicking. It's funny, you think, because she's so quiet when she isn't competing. That's not the case with Florida. She makes sure everyone hears her in and out of the ring. You get the impression that everything she says and does is for attention. Even now, as she loosens up with her team, she's moving with an assuredness that says, "Look at me, everyone. I'm the champ – and I can't be beat!"

"We'll see about that," you say under your breath and bite down on an energy bar.

You know Coach Kay wouldn't approve of these thoughts. He wants you to focus on your strategy and stay sharp by visualizing your fights – everything else is a waste of time. But you can't help it. You've been waiting all year for a rematch with Florida and still remember all the "what ifs" from your last fight. What if you moved a little faster? What if you blocked a little better? What if you landed one more kick? What if? What if? What if? And the ultimate what if – what if you didn't get caught by that sneaky roundhouse as time ran out. You also remember leaving the arena in tears, unable to stop thinking about how you let down your team, your coach, your family, even if they all said, "Good fight ... you'll get her next time."

You doze off, still listening to Beyoncé. And you're unsure how long you've been out when you feel a tap on the bottom of your foot.

"Time to get the blood flowing," Coach Kay says.

You start your warm-up routine by jumping rope, picking up speed quickly to let Texas know you saw her earlier and can outjump her in a heartbeat. She's watching. So is Idaho. But not Florida. She's stretching with her team and not paying attention to you or anyone else. You jump faster, the leather rope whirring by your head and tapping out a hurried beat as it barely slides through the fraction of an inch between the floor and the balls of your feet.

"Alright, that's good enough," Coach Kay says. "Save some energy for the ring."

"Yes, sir," you reply and finish with a last flurry of doubles.

Keep breathing, you remind yourself as you stretch to the right and left. With so much adrenaline pumping, it doesn't take long to loosen up. You bounce up and start with basic footwork drills, staying light on your feet as Coach Kay calls out the moves. Right foot in front. Left. Move forward. Back. Sidestep. Attack. Duck and counter. Attack again. You're moving like a shadow boxer now, dancing around your imaginary opponent and picking your shots. Looking over at Florida, you see she's going through a similar routine.

"Focus," Coach Kay says and slaps the target paddles.

"Yes, sir."

"There won't be any easy matches today," he adds.

Idaho's kicking paddles again – with those same sharp kicks you saw earlier – and she looks to have found a second wind. She's fast. But you're faster. Her kicks are strong. But yours are stronger.

"Watch her left leg," Coach Kay says. "She likes to set it up with a quick jab step."

You hit the target paddles, the snap of your padded feet on the paddles echoing off the walls. As you focus on each kick, you know others are watching. That's how it is in the holding area. Everyone's trying to pick up something they can use in the ring. Coach Kay throws a kick to keep you honest. It's a reminder not to forget about defense, though he mostly wants you to be on the attack.

"Match 94," announces the man on the PA. "Match 94. Bring your pads, your paperwork, and your coaches. You're going to Ring 1."

"Here we go," Coach Kay says. "It's showtime!"

You hold your blue chest protector – your *hogu* – against your body as Coach Kay ties the backstraps.

"Match 94," the man calls again. "You're going out."

A tournament official wearing yellow slacks and a matching long-sleeved shirt checks your hogu, your arm, shin, and foot pads, your headgear, your mouthpiece, and your nails. You'll grow them out when the tournament's over, you think. You might even paint them gold.

"Focus," Coach Kay says again and taps the sides of your hogu to let you know he's there.

"Yes, sir."

Now that you're standing beside Idaho, you notice she has a slight height advantage. That's not a problem, you think. You've beaten plenty of taller fighters over the years.

"Don't let her use her reach," Coach Kay whispers into the earhole of your helmet. "Get inside, stay inside."

I'm faster than her, you tell yourself.

"Get inside, stay inside."

"Yes, sir."

You bob your head left to right, in and out, listening to the cheers in the arena. When you glance one last time at Florida, she stops kicking and nods as if to say, "I'll see you later."

You nod back. Yes, you will.

"You got this," Coach Kay says.

"That's right," you say to your coach – and to yourself. "I've got this."

Marikina

It was the summer of 1944, nearly two years after the occupation began, when we received permission from the Office of the Military Governor to leave the city. As soon as father had the official paperwork, he loaded the horse-drawn *caratella* with our old canvas tent, some pots and pans and other household items from our apartment above his shop on Escólta Street, and a one-hundred-pound sack of rice. Other than the clothes on our backs, this is all we were allowed to take into the jungle near Marikina River.

"We'll return when MacArthur returns," father said on the night before we left Manila.

"Don't be naïve," uncle Lazarro replied. "Do you really think he gives a damn?"

"*Coño*," father snapped back. "I asked you not to talk like that around the boy."

Neither my uncle nor my father said another word, though I knew they were both mad.

Leaving early the next day, we arrived at our campsite a little before sunset, pitched our tent by an old banyan tree, and sat in silence around a small fire eating the last of the food mother had packed for the journey. Father set out at dawn the following morning, as he'd do every day during our time in the jungle, to look for food and gather firewood. Mother tidied up the campsite and spent the day preparing our meals, mostly grilled fish and chicken, yams and coconuts, mangos and papayas, and whatever else we could find in the jungle.

I also fell into a routine, attending classes at the makeshift school, finishing my homework under mother's watchful eye, and performing my assigned chores, such as sweeping out our tent with an old whiskbroom and carrying jugs of water from the river. We never ran into any soldiers, but the rumble of fighter planes overhead was a constant reminder of the war.

One day, after living in the jungle for nearly three months, I was surprised to see father return to camp leading a small pig by a leash.

"Here you go," father said, handing me the rope. "Take good care of him."

I named the pig Chato, after a dog we'd had before the war, and, in many ways, he was like a puppy. He'd splash in puddles, roll on his side for belly rubs, and spin around in circles with his snout in the air. I often took Chato for long walks in the nearby swamp, where he'd dig in the mud to root for grubs and worms. It didn't take long for me to fall in love with that little *baboy*. And everyone knew it.

"Here comes Pepe and his piglet," people would say.

"Those two are always together – like the Bobbsey Twins."

"You never see one without the other."

At night, I'd place Chato in a rusty metal cage next to our tent, where he'd burrow under an old blanket until only his nose and eyes were visible.

"*Buenas noches*, Chato," I'd whisper before shutting my eyes.

"*Buenas noches*, Pepe," I imagined him responding. "*Hasta mañana.*"

I often fell asleep to the sound of my pig snorting and snoring in his cage. And in the morning, when I pushed through the tent flaps, he'd press his snout against the grate, eager for food scraps or a taste of goat's milk. We lived like this for six months, with the pig growing fatter and fatter by the day, until one Sunday morning I awoke to find the cage open and Chato gone.

"Chato," I called. "Chato."

"*Bastos*," scolded my aunt Esmerelda from the campsite next to ours. "Did you forget we're hiding?" I lowered my voice and ran from one tent to the next asking if anyone had seen my pig.

"*Pobrecito*," mother said when I returned to camp with tears in my eyes.

"Chato is gone," I said, sniffling. "Will you help me find him?"

"Not now, *corazon*," she answered. "Wait for your father."

"But Chato …"

"Be patient," she said. "Sit and eat your breakfast."

"But …"

"Eat," she repeated and held out a bowl of rice topped by strands of red meat.

I did as I was told, though all I could think about was my pig. We should be looking for Chato, I thought as I chewed my food. Where's he run off to? What's going to happen to him? Why won't anyone help me? I wanted to ask again if I could look for my pig, but mother had a look on her face that said it was best not to bother her.

"Papa," I said when father returned to camp. "Chato is gone."

Father didn't say a word.

"Papa," I said again, pulling at his sleeve. "Chato isn't in his cage."

When father avoided my glance, I thought he must be upset at me.

"I'm sorry for leaving the gate unlocked."

"*Hijo*," he replied, "you didn't leave it unlocked."

"But how else could Chato escape?"

"You locked the gate," he said.

"How do you know?"

Father didn't answer me.

"How do you know?" I repeated.

"Stay here," he said. "I'll be back soon."

"Are you going to get Chato?" I asked, but father ignored me and walked into the jungle.

After finishing breakfast, I ran to the river to wash my bowl, my hands, and my face. I brushed my teeth and slicked down my hair before returning to camp to wait.

"Chato!" I called when father returned an hour later.

"I'm sorry, *hijito*," father said, "but Chato isn't coming back."

"What do you mean?" I asked as father handed me a string connected to a droopy red balloon. "What happened to Chato?"

"I'm sorry," father said again, "but we all have to make sacrifices."

"Chato!" I called as if my pig might come running if I yelled loud enough.

I slumped to the dirt, the droopy balloon at my feet, and sobbed like never before. I didn't want to hear about sacrifices. I didn't want to eat stale rice with stringy meat, or brush my teeth in a muddy river, or play with a red balloon, which I'd later learn was the inflated bladder of my pet pig. As I sat there crying, I wanted to run as far from camp as my feet would carry me. I wanted to return home to the city, even if it meant hiding from soldiers or being imprisoned – even if it meant never seeing my parents again. Most of all, I wanted my beloved pig. And nothing my father could say or do could ever change that.

It's the Water

When the time came to venture out after the blast, we drew straws to see who'd leave the cave to search for food – and to see what it was like out there.

*

We waited seven days after Zimmerman left before sending the next person.

After that, our wait times became shorter. Not because we were eager to leave the shelter of the cave, but because we didn't have a choice.

We were running out of food.

*

When we caught Breen stealing more than her share, we made her go next.

"Thief," Wilson shouted as we watched Breen leave.

"Traitor," yelled Singh.

At least there's one less mouth to feed, I thought, picking a piece of jerky from my teeth.

*

There were five of us left when I drew the short straw.

"It's a lot like Russian roulette," I said to the group.

I was bound to lose sooner or later.

We all were.

*

I buttoned my old coat, pulled my wool cap down tight, and made my way to the opening.

"See you soon," I called out to the others.

They nodded in agreement, though it was unlikely we'd meet again.

*

The first thing I noticed when I left the cave was the temperature.

It was surprisingly warm outside for the dead of winter. There should be snow on the ground, I thought, as I inhaled the warm, gritty air.

Something skittered to my left near a burnt-out chassis. I crouched in a defensive position and waited for whatever it was to come for me, though it never did.

*

After hiking for an hour or so, I spotted a clump of palm trees in the distance. The leaves swaying in the breeze beckoned me to walk on.

Is it a mirage? I wondered. A hallucination?

It wasn't until I heard the water that I knew it was real.

*

I broke into a sprint when I saw the pond and jumped in feetfirst without stopping to remove my clothes. The water was cool – refreshing.

After swallowing a few mouthfuls, I floated on my back and spat into the air like I was a fountain in the square.

*

I didn't see the bodies until I clambered out of the pond. There were all my predecessors. Zimmerman, Breen, Kramer, Singh, and the rest.

One by one they'd come the same way, lured by the trees … and the water.

"The water," I murmured, staring at the bodies in various states of decomposition.

Without warning, a jolt of pain in the pit of my stomach dropped me to the ground.

*

"It's the water," I wanted to scream so loud the others back in the cave could hear me.

But they were miles away, and my voice was barely a whimper, my last anguished gasps floating off on the hot, silent, radioactive breeze.

Operation Root Canal

The Commander ordered Rogers to take the bloody tooth to the lab for analysis and read aloud the handwritten note that had accompanied the grim package. "We'll send one tooth a day," read the scribbled message, "until you agree to our demands." From previous communications, we knew the kidnappers wanted five million dollars wired to an offshore account in the Cayman Islands. Only then would they provide the coordinates of the president's location.

"Follow me, Maxwell," the Commander said.

"Yes, sir."

A lanky man with long strides, the Commander led me down a dark hallway and into a wood-paneled, octagon-shaped room the size of a large walk-in closet. I braced myself when the floor began to drop, revealing the room to be a secret elevator.

"What you're about to see is highly classified," he said.

"Yes, sir."

The Commander led me down a dimly lit hallway and through a set of automatic doors that opened into a cavernous medical laboratory. A dozen or so people dressed in white coats, their faces covered by surgical masks, were working in different areas of the lab.

"Over here, Maxwell," the Commander said, leading me through a door marked "Authorized Personnel Only." Two guards positioned outside the door snapped to attention when we passed into the room.

After walking through another set of sliding doors, the Commander and I stepped into a smaller lab where two women, both wearing white coats and masks, were hunched over a stainless-steel table.

"Commander," they both said in muffled voices, but without looking up from their work.

"Come closer, Maxwell," the Commander ordered, gesturing for me to step toward the table.

It didn't take long to see what they were working on.

"But I thought the tooth was being analyzed in the main lab."

"Maxwell," the Commander said, motioning toward the two women. "I'd like to introduce you to Dr. Shabazz and her assistant, Special Agent Valery."

The doctor continued to examine the tooth, prodding it with a sharp metal instrument, the kind of tool a dentist uses for deep cleaning. Shabazz then exchanged the scraper for a long tweezer device.

"Here it is," she said, holding up a microprocessor.

"Excellent work, Shabazz," the Commander said. "Have the chip deciphered immediately. We can't put off their demands much longer."

The doctor placed the microprocessor on a metal tray held by Agent Valery. "Wait for the results," Shabazz instructed her assistant, "and report back as soon as you know anything."

Before Valery could leave the room, the door slid open and Rogers rushed in, holding a padded envelope.

"Sorry for the interruption, but we just received another package."

Rogers placed the envelope on the table.

"Open it," the Commander ordered.

Rogers cut open the envelope with a scalpel and poured out its contents. Two bloody molars rolled onto the table, leaving a pair of red smears on the stainless steel. The assistant removed a folded paper from the envelope and handed it to the Commander, who read the note aloud.

"'Surprise! Here are two more of your president's teeth. Hurry up with the ransom or we'll send something more substantial next time – maybe a finger or two.'"

"Bastards," Rogers cursed.

"They want to play dirty," the Commander said, "but this doesn't change our plan." He looked at Shabazz. "Add these two new teeth to the analysis."

"Yes, sir," said the doctor, quickly digging the microprocessors out of the teeth and placing them on Valery's tray. Meanwhile, the Commander turned his attention to Rogers. "Do what you can to stall them. We should know something soon."

The Commander, the doctor, and I watched in silence as Rogers and Valery left the room. When they were gone, Shabazz picked up one of the teeth and held it up to the fluorescent light.

"It's taken a long time to get to this point," the doctor said, "but we've finally perfected the procedure." She held the tweezers over a beaker of murky, burbling liquid, letting the tooth linger for a few seconds before dropping it into the substance, where it disintegrated immediately. She repeated the procedure with the other two teeth and removed her mask.

"Maxwell," the Commander said. "Let me introduce you again to Dr. Shabazz, one of our top counter-terrorism experts. Under her direction, we've launched phase one of a pilot program to infiltrate enemy strongholds in ways we never thought possible. We start the process by letting the enemy kidnap a high-level target."

"You're using the president as bait?" I blurted.

"What the enemy doesn't know," the Commander continued, "is that Dr. Shabazz has inserted these devices into the hostage's teeth, fitting each tooth with a powerful location tracker and audio-recognition sensor."

"We call it 'Operation Root Canal,'" Dr. Shabazz added.

"An important element of the operation," the Commander said, "is that we plant an agent within the enemy organization, someone who, with Dr. Shabazz's guidance, can pass as a torture expert specializing in tooth extraction."

"Someone to torture the President of the United States!" I exclaimed.

"Not exactly," the Commander replied. "You see, the hostage in this case isn't the president, but a surgically altered imposter."

"What?"

"You saw those people in lab coats in the other room," Dr. Shabazz explained. "We've recruited the nation's top medical experts, people like me who want to use their talents to make a difference. After identifying an agent with similar characteristics to a high-level kidnap target, we have everything we need to complete the perfect transformation."

The doors to the lab opened. "Here's the intel from the teeth," said Special Agent Valery. She handed a folder to the Commander. "We're ready to mobilize on your command."

"Excellent," the Commander replied. "Have the generals stand by in the war room."

"Yes, sir," Valery said and left again through the sliding doors.

"This is a great day for our organization – and for our country," said the Commander, flipping through the pages of the folder. "We're about to eliminate one of the world's most lethal terrorist groups once and for all."

"Congratulations, sir," said Dr. Shabazz.

"We couldn't have done it without you, Marlena," the Commander replied, continuing to review the folder. "I can't divulge the names in this report, but I can tell you that we've identified some very high-level people at the strike location." He shut the folder and turned his attention to me.

"Maxwell," he said, staring at me with his piercing gray eyes. "It's thanks to true patriots like Dr. Shabazz that we finally have the ability to do something about these terrorists."

The Commander tilted his chin to acknowledge the doctor while continuing to eye me with his steely stare. "And now, Maxwell, to the reason you're here."

I swallowed hard, waiting for the Commander to explain my role in this operation. I wanted to ask how he intended to extract the fake president and our torture specialist from the terrorist location, though I already knew the answer. We can always expect a certain amount of collateral damage in these types of situations, he'd say, echoing the Agency's motto: "This is what we sign up for."

"Here's the deal, Maxwell," the Commander continued. "You bear a resemblance to a billionaire arms dealer who's been the target of many kidnapping attempts by a large criminal organization, a group we've been trying to infiltrate for years."

Shabazz was staring at my mouth, as if sizing me up for an intricate dental procedure.

"With your help," the Commander continued, "we're ready to move ahead with phase two."

"You'll be known as a hero in these halls," Shabazz remarked, squeezing her hands into a pair of tight rubber gloves.

The Commander pressed a button hidden under the table and a half dozen security guards entered the room.

"They'll escort you to pre-op," said Dr. Shabazz, fitting a surgical mask over her face and grabbing a satchel of dental instruments.

"Like hell they will," I said, reaching for the scalpel on the table and pressing it hard against the doctor's throat. "If anyone tries to stop me, she'll be dead before she hits the ground." I looked at the Commander. "And that will be the end of your operation."

"Stand down," the Commander ordered the guards. "We need Shabazz alive."

"Here's what's going to happen," I said, leading Dr. Shabazz around the table. "I'm going to take the doctor with me to the front door. If anyone comes after us, I'll kill her."

"Think about what you're doing, Maxwell," the Commander said.

"I've thought about it," I replied. "And I'm getting out of here before you can place me – or some facelifted version of me – into a den of terrorists."

"We'll hunt you down, Maxwell," the Commander said as I led the doctor out of the room.

"I know you will, but you haven't left me with much of a choice."

I held the blade firmly against Shabazz's throat as we walked down the hallway and into the lab. Everyone's eyes were glued on the doctor and me as we passed through the room and made our way to the secret elevator.

"No sudden moves," I said to the doctor as the door slid open.

Once we reached the ground floor, I glanced back to make sure no one was following us before shoving Shabazz to the ground and fleeing headquarters. Don't look back, I told myself, as I sprinted across the street and descended into an underground subway station. Don't look back.

Fingers

Jimmy hired me to clean up the jobsite from time to time, though he mostly kept me around to be his drinking buddy. One day, after returning to work from one of our three-martini lunches, Jimmy was on the losing end of a gruesome encounter with a circular saw. I got lucky, however, when the cop who pulled us over on the way to the ER decided against giving me a sobriety test after I showed him Jimmy's severed fingers wrapped in my dirty, red bandana.

The Drummer

"Can we talk?" I asked the drummer who recently moved into the apartment above mine. "About what?" he replied. "Your drums are right above my bedroom," I told him. "And I haven't slept for days." He paused, shrugged his shoulders, and shut the door in my face. The next day, I drove to the sporting goods superstore for a 12-gauge shotgun, returned home, and waited for the drums to begin.

Serious as a Heart Attack

It's my first time back on the court since the heart attack. I should call it "my heart attack," but I can't bring myself to personalize the condition that nearly killed me two months ago. Thankfully, I feel good. I'm moving well and hitting the ball like the second coming of Roger Federer (okay, that's an exaggeration, but you get the point). Best of all, the pacemaker is purring like a new engine.

My wife, Jill, is on the other side of the net. She thinks I'm rushing back and should spend more time resting.

"Promise me you won't overdo it today," she said as we drove to the club.

"I'm fine," I told her. "Even Dr. McCumber recommended taking the new ticker for a test drive."

"We can stop at any time," she said. "Just say the word."

"Don't worry," I replied. "I know my limits."

Now that we're on the court, Jill is extending the time between rallies. She paces along the baseline for no good reason, takes a water break after nearly every rally, and keeps retying her laces.

"Let's pick up the pace," I say when we meet at midcourt to gather the balls hit into the net. "I'm not even sweating yet."

"Are you sure?"

"I'm a little out of breath," I tell her, "but only because of the time off. It doesn't have anything to do with the heart."

She cringes, like she always does when I talk about my condition in public, and sneaks a peek at the other courts to see if anyone heard me. On the court to our right, the retired veterinarian Simon Ruland and his wife are engaged in a feisty doubles match with the Whitcombs. To the right, the club's tennis pro is taking a group of kids through a series of conditioning drills.

"Don't worry," I say to Jill. "Simon can jumpstart my pacemaker if there's any trouble."

"I wish you wouldn't joke about it," she says.

"I feel great," I reassure her. "Let's play a set."

"That doesn't seem very smart."

"Come on," I say, "grant a dying man his last wish."

"That's not funny."

"Alright," I reply. "But let's play a quick set – the loser pays for dinner."

It's been nearly 20 years since we joined the club. As much fun as it is to play tennis, we also love the social aspect of our membership. We've developed some of our best and most lasting friendships with fellow club members. I'm still not a very good player, but I have a decent serve and never give up on a point. Jill, on the other hand, is highly skilled, having captained her team in college.

The longer I'm on the court, the better I feel. My backhand hasn't been this good in years, and my heart is holding up well under the exertion. After four games, we're tied at two apiece.

As Jill serves to start the fifth game, I get distracted by a familiar figure walking out of the clubhouse door and send my return sailing high over the fence. "Damn," I say, not because of the mishit, but because Misty Monroe is sauntering our way, wearing a hot-pink wraparound beach sarong held up by a red plastic clothespin.

"Hey Stuart," she says, stopping outside the fence. "Glad to see you're out and about."

"Nice to see you too, Misty," I mumble.

"Fifteen-love!" Jill shouts.

Her next serve is a rocket that whizzes by my flailing attempt to hit it.

"Thirty-love!" she shouts louder than before.

"Hey, she's good." Misty jumps up and down when she claps, each move jiggling her ample figure and putting that red clothespin at risk of popping off.

Now it's my turn to look at the other courts to see if anyone is watching us. Much to my dismay, the Rulands, the Whitcombs, and even the tennis pro and his students are staring in our direction.

Another serve rushes by.

"Forty-love!"

Misty claps again, but I don't dare to look, afraid of what might be revealed by further jiggling.

My wife smashes another ace.

"Game!" Jill roars, like Serena Williams on the verge of winning another major. Then she shouts for all to hear. "Tell that tramp to take a hike, Stuart, or I won't be so forgiving next time she gives you a heart attack."

Misty spins on her heels, her hot-pink sarong sashaying back to the clubhouse.

Sweat pours from my forehead and soaks through my polo shirt. I feel a slight flutter in my chest and wonder if the pacemaker is acting up.

"Your serve," Jill says, firing the balls over to my side of the court.

"We should probably go now," I reply. "I don't want to overdo it."

"We're almost done," she says. "Let's finish the set."

Bouncing on the balls of her feet, Jill pounces on my first serve with an intensity I haven't seen since her college days. From that point on, she unleashes one ferocious smash after another until I'm drawn, quartered, and defeated. My clothes are drenched, my hair is sopping, and my heart is racing like it might burst out of my chest at any second. Some test drive, I think while walking toward the net. When I open my mouth to congratulate Jill on her victory, she points a finger in my face.

"Don't say a word, you bastard. You owe me dinner."

The Dollhouse

You'd be 40 years old today, my age at the time of the first strike. There's some comfort knowing you didn't have to live through the disasters that came like seasons – drought, famine, disease, war, more war.

I awoke one morning without sight, which happened to many of us. We were placed in barracks according to our IQ. All blind, we ate as one. Slept as one. Felt as one.

Our power came slowly at first, before blossoming into full force. We'll use this incredible gift to improve things, I thought in the beginning. We'll create a better world. But the generals had other ideas.

When they no longer needed us for military purposes, they used us to keep the order. To keep the people in their place.

"Why didn't you revolt?" you would have asked. "Why didn't you turn your power against them?"

It's hard to explain, daughter, but we never thought to fight back. We never saw that as an option.

I still dream of you. Like last week when I saw you skipping toward me on a long sidewalk, your face bathed in sunshine as you made a point to avoid contact with the lines in the cement.

"Good girl," I cheered, "you're almost here."

"I'm coming, papa," you called out, though the distance grew between us.

"Faster, honey."

"Papa," you cried.

"Run!" I shouted.

I was jolted out of my dream by the familiar voice of G-5309.

"Silence," he commanded and struck the bottom of my feet with a metal baton.

Groans came from the other bunks in the barracks.

"Be quiet," he ordered. "Or you'll all get more of the same."

I willed myself back into my dream, but you were gone.

Did you look more like me or your mother? I can't remember anymore.

"No one's to blame," I told her. "It was just one of those things." But nothing convinced your mother to forgive – or to stay.

Last night, I dreamt you knelt before a two-story dollhouse, like the one we built together on your seventh birthday.

"My child," I said, tears welling in my eyes.

"Quiet, papa," you whispered.

Clutching my fists to my mouth, I peered over your shoulder at the dollhouse, only to realize that everything was covered by a thick, black ash, like the kind that fell on the last day I saw you.

"My child," I repeated, my words drowned out by the uncontrollable sobs coming from every bed in the room.

Like a Strange Song He'd Never Learn

"'*Salamat po*' means 'thank you,'" said Lola, attempting to teach Tagalog to her American grandson.

Gus couldn't even say those words without putting the accent on the wrong syllable.

"*Ay naku, corazon*! You'll never learn the language."

He butchered the phrase again and they laughed their heads off.

*

Gus was ten years old when he spent the summer with Lolo and Lola in Makati. It was his first time on an airplane. And the first time he ventured so far from home. At the departure gate at San Francisco International Airport, a Philippine Airlines flight attendant with long painted fingernails rested her hand on Gus's shoulder and promised his mother they'd take good care of the boy.

She kept her promise by bringing him bags of salted nuts and Coke after Coke after Coke.

*

It was dark and rainy when the plane landed. And the wind blew so hard the flags atop the terminal looked like they might rip away from their poles.

*

Lolo and Lola met Gus at the airport, and it wasn't long before they were inching along in traffic, with cars, buses, trucks, and jeepneys all around them. Even though it was raining hard, people walked through the traffic selling newspapers and magazines, fruit, candy, gum, and cigarettes.

"Keep your window up," Lola said.

"*Coño!*" Lolo cursed and pointed at a naked man urinating in the street.

"*Ay naku!*" Lola replied. "Don't look."

But it was too late. Gus had already seen all there was to see.

*

They'd go on long drives in the country to places like Baguio and Zamboanga and Tagaytay. "It's a lake within a volcano within a lake," a cousin said in a clipped accent that made Gus giggle.

*

One day, they drove for hours on a narrow, winding jungle road. Caribou stood in marshy groves, and large ferns reached into the roadway like long fingers.

Lolo told the driver to pull up in front of a hut where meat hung on the porch. It was dripping with blood as if the cows had just been slaughtered.

"Shall we have steak for dinner?" Lolo asked Gus.

"No, thank you," Gus said, but Lolo was already out of the car and motioning for his grandson to follow.

*

A man wearing a blood-smeared apron stepped onto the porch. He held a cleaver in one hand and a slab of meat in the other.

"What do you think of that cut?" Lolo asked.

The two men spoke in Tagalog and laughed when Gus backed away from the butcher.

"He says it's a good piece of meat," Lolo explained.

Gus was sweating so much his shirt stuck to his body.

"The boy might become a vegetarian," Lolo said to the butcher.

The two men laughed some more, and Gus felt his face redden.

"Come on now," Lola called from the car. "We should start back before dark."

The two men laughed harder when the butcher waved the raw slab under Gus's nose.

Lola spoke from the car again, more sharply this time and in Tagalog.

"Okay, okay," Lolo replied. "We're coming."

*

As they drove back to the city, Lolo chatted with the driver. Lola flipped through the pages of a fashion magazine. And the boy, while staring out at the palm trees and ferns, caribou and roadside shacks, wondered if he'd ever fit in to this country where everyone spoke a language that was like a strange song he'd never learn.

Transformation

The transport came in for a bumpy landing on Hos as the twin moons rose on the horizon. A medical technician by trade, Rael-6 had known this journey would come one day, though he worked hard to put it off. "It's just normal aches and pains," he'd say to anyone who asked about his condition. But those aches and pains had become worse, and, after a long consultation with Dr. Boethius, Rael-6 was forced to book his flight to the hospice planet.

"Seven hundred and fifty years is a good life," the admitting nurse remarked while checking his vital signs.

"Seven hundred and fifty-three to be exact," Rael-6 replied.

"A good, long life," the nurse said and smiled.

Rael-6 was soon sleeping and didn't stir until hearing a familiar voice whisper his name.

"Good morning," said Dr. Boethius. "How do you feel?"

"Old," Rael-6 answered. "How much more time do I have?"

"It's hard to say," the doctor answered. "We don't have a blueprint for these things."

"I see." Rael-6 settled back in his bed.

"Can I get you anything?" the doctor asked.

"No, thank you, doctor. I guess we'll just have to wait and see what happens next."

"That's the best approach." Dr. Boethius patted Rael-6's shoulder. "Don't hesitate to request more Doxa if you need it."

"Understood."

When Dr. Boethius returned three days later, Rael-6 was noticeably weaker. His skin was drawn tight over his entire body. And, as expected, there were large gashes on his torso.

"It won't be long now," the doctor said and administered a heavy dose of painkiller.

Rael-6 shut his eyes, a smile forming on his cracked lips.

Later that night, as Dr. Boethius was catching up on paperwork, a nurse hurried into his office. "It's Rael-6," she said. "It's time."

"Keep him sedated," the doctor ordered. "I'll be there in a few minutes."

"Yes, sir." The nurse telepathically administered more Doxa.

Rael-6 felt a warmth in his veins and was soon dreaming about being back home at his dining room table, sipping spice tea, and telling the doctor about a woman he'd met and the child he'd fathered while stationed on a mining ship in the Quadrillion galaxy.

"I begged the mother to stay with me," Rael-6 explained, "but she was committed to her career in deep space. I found out later that they both died in the Second Great Mining War."

"I'm sorry for your loss," the doctor said.

"I wouldn't have to do this alone if they had come with me." Rael-6 wiped a tear from his cheek.

"You're not alone," the doctor replied.

Rael-6 never woke from the dream. The hospice staff made sure of that as his tight, yellow skin, now covered in gashes, began to fall to the floor.

"Keep him fully sedated," Dr. Boethius ordered and peeled away a layer of skin.

A moan from the patient caused the doctor to glare at the nurse. "Fully sedated, I said."

"Yes, sir."

Rael-6 didn't make another sound as the doctor tore away more skin.

Ten days later, Dr. Boethius returned to find a new, young patient sitting up in bed.

"How do you feel?" the doctor asked.

"Like a million Napanthian crystals," answered the patient. "To tell you the truth, I'm not sure why I'm here."

"Just routine maintenance," Dr. Boethius assured him.

All is in order now, thought the doctor. Rael-6 is gone. In his place lay Rael-7, a fully rejuvenated Class-3Z model ready for deployment. This shell should last another 753 years, the doctor noted before prodding the patient's skin and checking his vitals one last time.

The Golden Buddha

There are times in life when you just can't say no.

Like the day Irving Lovelace stuck a 9mm Glock in my face. As it turned out, my old cellmate wanted my help with a job at a club on Grant Street, the place with the golden Buddha shrine. I've always liked the way the Buddha stares into your eyes as if he can see right into your soul. But I never thought of the statue as anything more than an odd curio until Irving showed up and told me it was made of solid gold and crafted during the Ming Dynasty.

"Put the gun away, Irv," I told him that day. "I'm in."

I got the ball rolling by hiring a top-notch crew. Well, as top-notch as you can get these days. We needed an experienced driver, so I called Stan Silverado in Los Angeles. Once a hotshot Hollywood stuntman, Stan was on the outs in Tinseltown after having an affair with the director's wife during a film shoot. For muscle, I had to go with Irving, though I brought Toots Underbelly onboard for backup. (I told him to keep an eye on Irv and feed him to the sharks out by the Farallons if I disappeared under mysterious circumstances.) Last, I rang up Buffy Stonebreaker, a secret weapon if there ever was one. Buffy and I had been an "item" back in the day, though she dropped me faster than a white-hot horseshoe when I was sent to the slammer. I didn't know who my old flame was seeing now, and I didn't care. All that mattered was that Buffy's the best in the business when it comes to disabling alarms.

We pulled up in front of the club at a little past three o'clock in the morning, knowing it would be closed until the cleaners arrived at six.

"Here you go, Stan." Buffy handed our driver a brown paper bag. "It's just a couple of bear claws to snack on while you wait. I made them this afternoon."

"Thanks, doll," Stan said and dug into the pastries.

That's odd, I thought, remembering back to the time Buffy tried to bake a cake for my birthday and nearly burnt down the house. I guess we can all develop new talents over time, I told myself while falling into step with the others.

After I picked the lock on the front door, Buffy worked on the alarm. She moved like a cat, slinking against the wall until she found the control panel. I have to admit I was starting to get that old feeling for her again. Hey, nothing says "potential for rekindled romance" better than pulling off a heist together, right? Anyway, after about ten minutes, Buffy gave the all-clear sign and switched on the overhead lights.

"Come to papa," I said, striding toward the shrine.

"Wait," Buffy said in an urgent whisper.

"What's the matter?"

She came toward me, with those cat-like moves again, grabbed a pair of wire cutters from her tool bag, and snipped a thick black wire at the base of the statue.

"It's a backup alarm," she said and returned the cutters to her pouch.

"That was close," I replied, a grin stretching across my face. And that's when I saw Toots crack down hard on Irv's skull with the butt of his gun. "What the hell?" I stepped toward the muscleman.

"Hold it right there, sweetie," Buffy called out.

I turned to see my old girlfriend pointing a pistol at me.

"What's going on here?"

"It's like this, lover boy." Toots wrapped his arm around Buffy's waist. "Me and Buffy are grabbing this haul for ourselves."

I stared at them, from one to the other and back again, my brain trying to process the notion that Buffy and this goon had been planning their own caper.

"A double-cross?" I muttered in disbelief.

"Take it easy, Ferguson," my ex instructed, "and you won't get hurt."

"Except for your pride," Toots snickered.

Still giggling as he crossed the room, Toots was making a beeline toward the gold Buddha when his attention was drawn to the cash register on the counter.

"We could use a little spending money for the road, don't you think?"

Before Buffy could answer, Toots pressed the button to open the register drawer. In the next instant a piercing shriek caused us all to groan. Buffy had shut off the backup alarm for the Buddha, but not for the cash register.

As Toots and Buffy held their hands to their ears, I fought through the pain and scrambled out of the club, leaving the lovebirds behind to deal with the statue and whatever else came their way. I hurried to the van, only to learn that Buffy had been up to more of her tricks. The bear claws she'd baked for Stan were laced with something that knocked him out for good.

Setting out on foot, I took advantage of the early-morning darkness to hide in the shadows as the howl of approaching sirens reverberated through the empty city streets. With any luck, I thought, I'll get to the Greyhound station in time to buy a one-way ticket for somewhere as far away as possible from those dishonest crooks and that damned golden Buddha.

Skunk

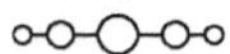

It was three o'clock in the morning when I saw the skunk. It was dark out except for splashes of light from the construction site. Maybe she'd wriggled under the fence, I thought. Was she looking for food? Or did she have something else in mind? That old cartoon flashed into my head – frisky Pepé le Pew in hot pursuit of the black cat, her back streaked white by the inadvertent swipe of a painter's brush. "Mind if I join you?" I asked while crossing the street with my tail in the air.

44 Seconds

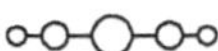

I ate lunch every day with a co-worker named Bob.
We'd meet at the microwave to cook frozen eggrolls
from the vending machine. The instructions were
simple: "Heat on both sides for 45 seconds each."
I noticed that Bob always cooked his rolls for 44
seconds. Not 45. One day, when I asked him why,
he watched the timer run down, pulled the steaming
eggroll out of the microwave, and looked me in the eye
before saying, "Obama."

Long Long Gone

Spike stared at the fork in the road, hoping an answer might come if he looked long and hard enough. Would she have taken the high road, he wondered, or the low? Sitting on a charred stump, Spike kicked off his left boot and removed the silver dollar he kept tucked beneath the insole. The coin was a parting gift from his old man on the day he left for good.

"Heads, I take the high road," he said. "Tails, the low."

Spike flipped his lucky coin, snatched it out of the air with a flourish, and slapped it on the back of his hand. The high road it was.

*

I don't know what it is about that guy, thought Marla-Jean as she pulled the '68 Chevelle into a spot in front of the Lazy Day Market, but he damn sure gets under my skin sometimes. She bought a pack of Kools from the pimply-faced teen in the store, crossed the road to the diner, and ordered a cheeseburger.

Sitting at a table by the window, Marla-Jean stared out at the sylvan scene, with the sun shining through the branches and the warm breeze blowing through the leaves. This could be a nice place to live, she thought, though her mind kept flashing back to Spike's hairbrained idea from earlier in the day.

"One last job," he said. "Then we're done for good."

"Why push our luck?" Marla-Jean asked. "We barely got away from the last job."

"Just give it some thought." Spike walked into the woods to heed nature's call. "I'll be back in a minute," he said over his shoulder.

By the time he returned, Marla-Jean was gone.

*

"Need a lift?" a friendly voice hollered from a brown pickup.

"Much obliged." Spike jumped in. And it wasn't long before the truck was rolling into a small town made up of a handful of vacation rentals, a gas station, a market, and a diner.

"I'll be getting out here," Spike said to the driver when he spotted Marla-Jean. "Thanks for the ride."

After watching Spike take a few nervous steps, Marla-Jean flashed a toothy smile and motioned for him to pick up the pace.

"That's my girl," Spike said.

*

"What took so long?" Marla-Jean asked when Spike joined her at the table.

"It's a long way from the middle of nowhere," Spike said before turning serious. "I'm sorry about earlier."

Marla-Jean shrugged. "You caught me off guard, that's all."

Spike looked into Marla-Jean's dark-brown eyes, waiting to see what she'd say next.

"Were you serious?" she asked.

"About what?"

"About doing one last job."

*

Marla-Jean painted her toenails, the chemical smell of the polish filling the car even though the windows were down. As much as Spike hated the smell, he kept his mouth shut and his eyes on the road. We'll get to the bank soon enough, he thought. No need to rile her up now.

*

The smell of the nail polish was gone – and all squabbles were forgotten – by the time they reached the bank. Spike pulled a black mask over his head. Marla-Jean scrunched her hair into a ponytail and covered her face with a flesh-colored stocking.

"Here's to our last job," she said even though Spike was already out of the car.

*

"Get down on the floor," Spike shouted, "and no one gets hurt." The slap of his hand on a desk echoed off the vaulted ceiling.

Marla-Jean leveled her gun at the bank manager.

"Fill it with hundreds," she ordered, tossing him an old canvas bag.

The manager's nervous eyes gave Marla-Jean the impression that he might bolt for the door at any moment.

"Play it cool," she said, "and we'll be gone faster than you can say 'lickety-split.'"

*

"Well, that was a piece of cake." Spike checked the rearview mirror to make sure no one was following them.

"A big, moist hunk of chocolate cake."

Spike grinned. "Maybe we should do another one since we're on such a roll?"

"You're funny," Marla-Jean said and laughed. And she continued to laugh until the moment she pulled a wad of bills from the bag. "What the hell?"

"What's wrong?"

When Marla-Jean remained silent, Spike pulled the car off the road and reached into the bag. "Those bastards," he said, flipping through a bundle of fake bills. "They were on to us the whole time."

He tossed the bag into the backseat and whipped the car around.

"What are you doing?" Marla-Jean asked.

"We have some unfinished business at the bank," Spike replied. "That's what I'm doing."

*

Two news trucks were on the scene. And three police cars. Spike pulled his cap down low on his forehead as they drove by.

"Are you crazy?" Marla-Jean said after they rounded a corner.

"Relax," Spike answered. "We'll wait for it to get dark and then get what we came for."

He tucked the car into a shady spot behind the bank and leaned his chair back.

Marla-Jean pulled a small mirror from her purse and checked her hair. "I'll never understand how you can sleep at a time like this."

"We all need our beauty rest, darling." Spike looked over at Marla-Jean and winked. "Wake me in an hour."

*

It was quiet out when they broke in through the back door.

"Who'd have thought we'd be hitting the same bank twice in a day?" Spike said.

"Let's get this over with," Marla-Jean replied and began stuffing hundred-dollar bills into the bag.

Wandering off to see what else he might find, Spike hurried back a few minutes later. "When you finish with the cash," he said, his voice noticeably excited, "leave the bag by the door and help me with the gold."

"Gold?"

"Yeah, there's a bunch of gold bars in the other room."

"We don't have time for gold," Marla-Jean snapped. "Let's stick to our plan."

"I'd say our plan changed about the time they slipped us those phony bills," Spike replied.

*

After stacking the last gold bar on a metal cart, Spike lowered his shoulder and pushed. When the cart didn't budge, he heaved again, figuring he just needed a little momentum to get the wheels moving.

"Leave it," Marla-Jean implored.

Before Spike could respond, a blinding light shone through the window.

"Come out with your hands up," a man's voice boomed over a bullhorn.

Spike pulled his gun from his waistband.

"Spike, don't!" Marla-Jean cried, but it was too late.

*

When the shooting stopped, Spike lay sprawled on the floor, a pool of blood forming from a gunshot wound in his chest.

Marla-Jean crouched behind a desk, looking from one side of the room to the other, thinking about her next move.

"Come on out," bellowed the man on the bullhorn. "We'll give you a fair chance."

"You call this a fair chance?" Marla-Jean muttered as she looked over at Spike for the last time and lifted her gun.

Another blaze of gunfire lit up the bank.

*

Walking toward the light, Spike and Marla-Jean soaked in the cheers of everyone who'd come to see the famous bank robbers, the young couple whose faces were splashed all over the papers.

"We're famous," Marla-Jean whispered as she scanned the crowd. She saw the man with the bullhorn, the nervous bank manager, the pimply-faced kid from the market, and the rest of the crowd.

"Look over there, honey." Marla-Jean pointed to a familiar figure across the street.

Standing alone in a doorway, Spike's old man flipped his lucky coin high in the air, snatched it with a dramatic flourish, and nodded for them to come over.

It was tails.

Game Crazy

When I left home a few hours ago, dad was settled into his favorite spot on the couch, swigging beer and pumping himself up for the start of a basketball game on television.

"This is it," he cheered when I entered the room.

"This is what?" I asked.

"Game seven of the NBA Finals," he explained, elongating each syllable like he was explaining a complex math problem to a toddler. "Tonight, we bring home the championship."

"Sounds good," I said, knowing he'd never understand my disinterest in sports.

He crumpled the empty can and threw it toward the wicker trash basket at the end of the couch. "Aaaaaiiiirrrbbbaaalll!" he shouted when the can clattered on the floor.

"I'll be home after the play," I said. "It shouldn't be too late."

"Take your time," he replied and pulled another can from the cooler. "I'm not going anywhere."

By the time I arrived at the playhouse, I'd put dad out of mind and was ready to enjoy *One Flew Over the Cuckoo's Nest*. If you've seen the play (or more likely the movie), you probably recall the scene where the patients, led by Randle McMurphy, petition Nurse Ratched to let them watch the World Series.

The baseball game is scheduled during a time when the TV is off limits, and the only way the patients can watch is by voting to change the rules. McMurphy eventually succeeds in getting a unanimous show of hands, only to have the nurse reach into her bag of dirty tricks to invalidate the vote.

Undeterred, McMurphy gathers the men in front of the screen and invents an imaginary play-by-play of the action taking place on the field. Soon, everyone in the ward is cheering a shared field-of-dreams fantasy.

After the play, I stopped by Lottie's for a cup of coffee and a slice of cherry pie. I was about halfway through the pie when I remembered to turn my phone back on and check my messages.

"Hello," an unfamiliar voice began. "This is Officer Lynch of the Fountainview PD. Everything is fine, but I wanted to let you know that your father was picked up tonight. I won't go into detail. Let's just say that things got a little out of control and he was transported to Our Lady of Angels psychiatric hospital for observation."

I stared at the phone, dumbfounded and unsure about what to do next. I listened again, keying in on certain phrases … "your father was picked up … out of control … psychiatric hospital."

"Crap!" I said aloud and asked for the bill.

Dad was no stranger to medical facilities. In the last three years alone, he'd undergone a back procedure, knee-replacement surgery, and the removal of his gallbladder.

"Let's see what the butchers want now," he'd joke any time I took him to see a doctor.

But a psychiatric hospital, really?

He was fast asleep when I entered the room, with his arms and legs restrained and a thick black belt strapped across his chest.

What the hell's going on here? I thought. I need to find the doctor. When turning to leave the room, however,

I spotted the clipboard at the bottom of the bed. It included a few scribbled notes.

... found roaming outside ... naked except for socks ... clear signs of inebriation ... refused assistance ... hurled insults ... it took two officers to subdue him ... even after tazing ...

"Jesus," I muttered. "Tazing?"

A whimper came from the bed.

"Dad, what happened?"

He shut his eyes.

"What happened?" I said again.

He cracked his eyelids open for an instant before shutting them again.

"Are you okay?"

He shrugged.

I patted him on the shoulder. "We can talk about it tomorrow."

Dad opened his eyes again and motioned with his chin for me to come close.

"What is it?"

"It was the game," he moaned.

"What about the game?"

"We had it in the bag."

"And ...?"

"It was the worst fourth-quarter collapse in playoff history," he said, tears streaming from his eyes.

He turned his head to avoid my disbelieving stare. And, for once in my life, I wished with all my heart I could understand why he loved that stupid game.

Aftershock

Orchestra center. Front row.

Before the earthquake, Gus had season tickets to the
symphony. It had been his one splurge in life – front
row center. He was such a regular back then the ushers
and bartenders knew him by name. But that was long
ago. Now, on the rare occasions when Gus treated
himself to a concert, he sat in the uppermost reaches of
the balcony.

Listening to the musicians tune their instruments,
Gus, who was approaching his eighty-third birthday,
remembered back to the time when he knew them all
by sight – the ruddy-cheeked cellist, the elegant harpist,
and the exquisite violinist with long fingers and silky
black hair that shined under the glimmer of the stage

lights. Where has she gone? Gus wondered as the conductor lifted his baton. Where have they all gone?

With the orchestra poised to play, Gus peeked at his old seat in the front row.

It was empty.

*

Back in 1989, when the quake hit, Gus was wrapping up his day's work as a legal clerk on the thirty-third floor of a downtown San Francisco office building. Having been raised in the city, Gus was accustomed to seismic activity – but nothing like this. Afraid the building might collapse, the clerk dropped to his knees and prayed for the shaking to stop. That's the position he was in when Reggie Stimpson, the firm's accountant, rushed into the room.

"Gus!" Reggie reached for Gus's shoulders to steady himself. "We need to talk!"

"What do you mean?" Gus replied. "We need to get out of here."

"Just listen to me for a minute."

Reggie had a disconcerting way of speaking in which his eyes bulged as if he were in a state of perpetual astonishment. Like Gus, Reggie had worked at the firm for ten years. Also like Gus, Reggie liked everything about the job except the low pay.

"Listen to me," Reggie said again, his eyes wider than usual. "You know how Leon locks the safe every night before leaving."

As the tremor subsided, Gus stood and grabbed his coat.

"You can't leave, Gus!"

Something about the urgency in Reggie's voice stopped Gus. "Alright," he said, "I'm listening, but make it quick."

"Here's the deal." Reggie took a deep breath before continuing. "Leon was the first to leave the building when the quake hit."

"Sounds like he had the right idea."

"Yes, except for thing." Reggie's eyes were nearly bursting out of his head. "He forgot to shut the safe."

"Go on," Gus said.

"I'm not saying we take it all." Reggie lowered his voice before continuing. "But we have a once-in-a-lifetime opportunity right now to give ourselves a little bonus."

A little bonus, Gus thought. He liked the ring of that.

*

If Gus had looked out the floor-to-ceiling window in Leon's office, he would have seen fire and smoke in the Marina. Instead, his eyes were glued on a corner of the room where the open safe was illuminated by a faint sliver of light.

"There must be a couple million dollars in there," Gus figured.

Reggie nodded. "And no one will know if we grab a few bucks for ourselves."

"I don't know, Reg."

"Come on," the accountant urged. "It's foolproof."

Gus turned toward Reggie. "You could have taken the money for yourself. Why are you getting me involved in this?"

"Because you used to work in the mailroom, right?"

"So?"

"So, you know how to work the postage machine."

Reggie was right about that. Gus could operate the mailroom equipment in his sleep.

"Why don't we just fill our briefcases and walk out the door? Why do we need to put the money in the mail?"

"We don't know what's happening out there," Reggie answered. "There could be chaos in the streets." Reggie knelt in front of the safe and began stuffing cash into a large envelope. "I'm telling you, Gus, no one will ever know."

"And it'll probably be days before they even realize it's gone," Gus mused.

"Now you're talking, partner."

*

The two thieves quickly found a rhythm. Reggie stuffed, addressed, and sealed envelopes, while Gus hustled back and forth from the mailroom where he weighed and stamped the packages before dropping them into the mail chute. The office was quiet except for the hum of the emergency generator, the mechanical clicks of the stamp machine, and the heavy whoosh of envelopes sliding down to the collection bin in the basement.

It was nearly midnight when Gus dropped the last package in the chute. "Alright," he said to Reggie, "let's get out of here."

"Hold on," Reggie replied. "We need to do one more thing."

"What are you talking about?"

"We need an alibi." Reggie was on the move now, leading Gus down the corridor, back toward the accounting department.

"An alibi?"

"Yeah, an alibi in case anyone asks why we didn't leave with everyone else." The accountant turned to look

Gus in the eye. "We're going to make it look like I was injured during the quake."

"Are you crazy?"

"Not at all." Reggie strode into his office, opened the top drawer of his desk, and pulled out a small baseball bat, the kind you might get as a souvenir at the ballpark.

"What's that for?" Gus asked.

"First, we're going to turn this office upside-down. We'll knock over all the furniture. We'll scatter files and papers and supplies everywhere." Reggie paused to strike the bat against his palm. "And then you'll make it look like I was hurt."

"You are nuts!"

"No, Gus. Like I said before, this is foolproof."

Reggie tossed the bat to Gus and began to trash his office.

*

Reggie started with the large bookshelf. He flung the contents of each shelf onto the floor and pulled down the heavy piece of furniture. Then he emptied the file cabinets and desk drawers, flinging papers and everything else around the room. When he was done, Reggie, his eyes bulging, pointed to a spot above his left eyebrow.

"Okay slugger. Give it to me right here."

"What are you talking about?" Gus asked.

"Just hard enough to cause a small bump."

"I can't do it, Reg."

"I'm telling you. We need an alibi."

"I know, but this is wrong."

"Hit me!" Reggie shouted.

"Reggie, I ..."

"Hit me!" he yelled louder.

Gus tapped the bat lightly against the side of Reggie's head.

"That's not going to cut it."

Gus hit him again.

"Harder!"

Gus did as he was told.

"One more time," Reggie slurred.

Gus whipped the bat down on Reggie's skull, the force of the blow snapping the handle and dropping the accountant to the floor.

*

Stepping toward the doorway, Gus was ready to get as far away as possible from the office when he looked back at Reggie. "Get up. Get up. Get up," Gus whispered while scanning all the clutter. It was only when his eyes landed on a framed picture of Reggie and his wife Rachel on their Caribbean honeymoon that Gus began to calm down.

Gus had met Rachel at company events over the years. And Gus always thought of Reggie's wife as attractive. But he never appreciated the full extent of her beauty until he was staring at this vacation photo. "You lucky dog," Gus muttered and nudged the accountant with the toe of his shoe. "Let's get you home to this enchantress."

When Reggie didn't stir, Gus crouched and poked him in the back.

"Come on, Reg," he said. "It's time to wake up."

Gus prodded and poked and shook Reggie until finally realizing the accountant wasn't going anywhere – that last swing of the bat had caused more than a temporary knockout.

To this day, Gus doesn't know what inspired his next move. All he could think about in the panic of the moment was making the accident look as real as possible. So, after lifting the heavy bookshelf to waist level, Gus positioned the top edge over Reggie's skull.

"Sorry, Reg," Gus said before releasing his grip on the heavy piece of furniture.

*

At intermission, Gus stayed in his balcony seat, his memory on overdrive. He remembered walking alone down thirty-three flights of stairs, tossing the broken bat into the Bay, and explaining the "terrible accident" to a policeman who took down all the information in a little black notebook before telling Gus to go home.

In the end, everyone believed Gus's story that Reggie had simply been in the wrong place at the wrong time. As for the stolen money, Gus's portion showed up in the mail exactly as Reggie planned. And when Gus eventually returned to work, no one said a word about the missing cash. It wasn't just that the money disappeared; it was like it never existed in the first place.

Reggie had been right – the plan was foolproof.

*

In the months after the quake, Gus couldn't stop reliving the events of that night. The jolt. The panic. The screams. The prayers. The swaying building. The bug-eyed accountant. The envelopes. The mail chute. The bat. The bookshelf. Still, one memory stood out from the rest. Gus became obsessed with the framed picture of Reggie and Rachel on their honeymoon. Specifically, he couldn't get Reggie's bombshell of a wife out of his mind. Finally, on the six-month anniversary of the quake, Gus arranged to meet her.

"Come on in." Rachel greeted Gus with a friendly kiss on the cheek. "Can I get you a drink?"

Now, after all the waiting, and after imagining over and over what he'd say when they finally met, Gus was at a loss for words. Dressed in a sparkling red gown, Rachel was even more beautiful than he remembered – even more beautiful than in the photograph.

"What's the matter, Gus? Cat got your tongue?"

"No, I ..." Gus eyed her shimmering low-cut dress.

Rachel leaned in before Gus could formulate a sentence. "Cut the crap," she said. "I know why you're here."

*

As Gus soon learned, Rachel knew a lot more about the money than he did.

Not long before the quake, while Reggie was travelling for work, Rachel had a weekend tryst with an old beau – a guy who worked as a bodyguard for the mob. When she told her mob boyfriend about Reggie's position at the firm, he let her in on a little secret that his boss used the same firm to launder cash.

Careful not to reveal her source, Rachel eventually passed on this tidbit to Reggie, planting the idea that he might be able to give himself a nice little bonus someday. "You deserve it, honey," she whispered one night while nibbling his ear.

"How did you know I was involved?" Gus asked when Rachel finished her story.

"As you know," Rachel explained, "Reggie was someone who was always thinking ahead. So, on the night when you stole the money, he left a note in one of the envelopes, telling me about the plan and to keep an eye out for you if anything happened to him."

"So, what's our next move?" Gus asked.

"I don't know about our next move," Rachel replied, "but your next move is to hand over the rest of the cash."

"Why would I do that?"

"Because I've gotten back together with my old boyfriend – the one who breaks bones for a living – that's why."

*

A tingling in Gus's left arm was followed by a shooting pain in his neck. The musicians were playing now, though Gus barely heard them. Rubbing his arm, the old man tried to ignore the pain by focusing his attention elsewhere. That's when he realized that someone had finally taken his old front-row seat.

"Who's there?" he wondered. "Who's in my seat?"

Another jolt, more painful than the first, hit Gus when he recognized the man.

"Impossible," he muttered

Gus slumped down in his seat when Reggie turned to wave. Rachel was there too, dressed in the shimmering gown she wore all those years ago. "Impossible," Gus repeated when noticing the orchestra was also filled with familiar faces – the ruddy-cheeked cellist, the elegant harpist, the silken-haired violinist, and the rest. They all stood and waved toward the balcony.

"Bravo," Gus whispered as he clutched his chest. "Well played."

Shut Up and Write

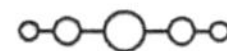

"Let the writing begin," says the man at the head of the long wooden table.

Fourteen writers, a group that meets every Wednesday morning for three and a half hours, have come to the Owl and Monkey Café to write. Just write. Nothing else. No phone calls. No texts. No email. No internet. And above all else – no talking.

After three minutes of silence, there's a commotion near the front door. Some writers turn up the volume of the music piping into their ears. Others look up from their laptops to see a woman rushing toward the table.

"Is this the writing group?" she asks in a breathless voice. "Sorry I'm late."

Benmont Stimpson, the poet who leads the group, motions for the newcomer to take an empty seat. The woman, her name is Jolene Montegrosso, pulls a chair from the table, the legs scraping loudly on the hardwood floor.

"Sorry, sorry, sorry," she says to the group.

As the writers settle back into their work, Jolene drops her bulky black leather purse on the floor, plops into her chair, shifts forward with another loud scrape, and tears open the Velcro flap on her backpack.

By this time the writers are fidgety, waiting for Benmont to say something.

"Sshh," he whispers.

"What?" Jolene whispers back.

Before Benmont can respond, Jolene sneezes three times, each one louder than the previous, and all of which cause further ripples of unrest among the group. Just when it seems like she's done, Jolene uncorks the Mother of All Sneezes, rummages for a handkerchief from her purse, and blows her nose with a thunderous honk that reverberates off the café walls. When things finally quiet down, and when the writers are working again, Jolene starts to tap her fingernails on the table while waiting for her laptop to boot up – which it eventually does with an annoying whoosh.

Barney Flaharty, an ornery old essayist writing about gun violence in the workplace, clears his throat. "Excuse me," he says. "But this is a quiet space."

Two writers "sshh" Barney.

"Don't 'sshh' me," he tells them. "I'm not the one making all the noise."

"Okay, everyone." Benmont pauses the timer. "Let's take a moment to go over the ground rules."

Sighs are heard around the table as the writers must again pause in mid-stream. Tanya Bellwether, a biographer putting the finishing touches on her book about the life and times of Charles Bukowski, mutters a string of expletives.

"Here's the deal," says Benmont. He's speaking to the group but staring straight at Jolene. "The concept is simple. We come together once a week to escape the distractions of our busy lives. We come together to write essays and articles, novels and short stories. And, yes, some of us even come to write poetry. But, most importantly, we all come together on these precious Wednesday mornings to shut up and write!" Benmont blushes when the words come out harsher than intended.

After taking a deep breath, the poet continues, "Let's get back to work, shall we?"

"Excuse me …" It's Jolene.

"Yes."

"I want to get something straight." If Jolene's picked up on the anger coming from the group, she doesn't show it. "Does this mean we can't talk … at all?"

"Oh my god," blurt Tanya Bellwether and Barney Flaharty at the same time.

"That's right," Benmont answers, struggling to keep calm. "No talking at all."

"Got it." Jolene smiles and makes a motion of buttoning her lips with her thumb and forefinger.

Things finally settle down. And everyone at the table – including Jolene – focuses on their writing. This is how is should be, thinks Benmont, when he looks up from the persona poem he's composing to see all of the writers perched over their laptops. He grins while thinking of words to describe the scene: "creative," "productive," "serene," and, best of all, "quiet." He's about to dig back into his poem when something catches his eye from the far corner of the table. It's Jolene waving to get his attention.

"What now?" Benmont asks.

Jolene points toward her lap.

"What?"

"I know we're not supposed to talk," she says, "but I need to go to the bathroom."

"Give me a break," Trevor Sedgewick groans. He's a science-fiction author penning the sequel to his post-apocalyptic novel in which San Francisco has been overrun by a giant man-eating silverfish.

"I need to go to the bathroom," Jolene repeats, enunciating each word.

"Really?" Trevor replies. "Does this look like kindergarten to you?"

"Steady, Trev," says Benmont. "I have this."

"Like hell you do," snarls Angus Tremaine, a city councilman who blogs about Rottweilers in his spare time.

"I have to go now," Myra Spritzneck announces to the group. She's a podiatrist writing a romance novel set in a Montego Bay resort at the height of hurricane season. "I can't possibly concentrate with all this racket."

"Wait a minute, Myra," Benmont pleads.

But Myra has already packed up her laptop and is on her way out the door.

"See you next week," Benmont calls out more as a question than a statement.

"Sshh," scolds Barney, wagging his finger like an agitated librarian.

Jolene waves her hand again. "Um … excuse me."

"What?" Benmont shouts.

"Can I go to the bathroom now?"

"Yes," says Benmont. "No one cares when you pee. Just get up quietly and go."

Two more writers put away their things. Benmont raises a hand to stop them, but they brush past the poet and don't look back.

"Hey," Jolene calls out while walking to the bathroom, "where are they going?"

Benmont's only response is to glare at Jolene, and he's still glaring when she returns to the table, again scraping her chair across the hardwood floor.

With an air of disruption hanging over the group, a political satirist named Chester W. Mulroney rises from the table and storms off without saying a word. Everyone watches Chester leave – everyone except Jolene, that is. Headphones on. Eyes glued to her monitor. She types furiously – and loudly – about a cat named Frisco LaGrange who was recently adopted by the owner of a tropical fish store.

Thinking he's died and gone to cat heaven, Frisco spends most of the day lounging on a comfortable old recliner, though he's not sleeping. No, instead the wily feline is busy hatching an elaborate plan to snatch goldfish from the shop's well-stocked aquariums. After a couple of weeks, and after Frisco has put on a few pounds, the shop owner beams with happiness, seeing how his cat has settled in so nicely to life at the store. As time goes on, however, the owner begins to suspect foul play.

Jolene types faster and harder, her fingers like little pistons on the keyboard as she drives toward her story's climax. Just as she's ready to describe the shop owner's scheme to catch Frisco red-handed (so to speak), a buzzer rings at the head of the table.

"Time's up," Benmont announces.

"Thank god," blurts Sadie Hill, who, under the penname Majestic Ambrosia, writes futuristic flash fiction set on an intergalactic sex colony. She packs up quickly and leaves, with the others following suit. Soon, the only writer left at the table is Jolene, who's still pounding away on the keyboard.

"Excuse me," says Benmont.

Jolene doesn't look up.

"Excuse me," Benmont says again and taps Jolene on the shoulder.

She lifts her headphones off her ears. "Can't you see I'm writing?"

"Yes, but it's time to wrap it up."

"Just a few more minutes. I'm almost done."

"Sorry," says Benmont, "I have to move all the furniture."

"Oh well." Jolene powers down her laptop. "I'll finish this gem at home."

Benmont ignores her while rearranging the tables and chairs.

After packing up, Jolene turns toward Benmont. "Same time next Wednesday?"

Benmont almost answers "yes" but pauses instead to see if any of the other writers are still in the café. "Actually," he says, leaning close, "we're moving to Mondays starting next week."

"Glad I asked," Jolene calls over her shoulder. "I'll see you then."

"Sounds good," Benmont replies while sliding a chair across the hardwood floor and turning his head to hide the mischievous chuckle forming in his throat.

Acknowledgments

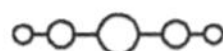

Special thanks to the following for their contributions.

Dan Davis	For his careful reading. And for interior page layout.
Richard Osborn	For his photo of the author.
Aimee Stevland	For her cover design.
Cristina Deptula	For spreading the word for authors, large and small.
Rosalie Lack	For being my constant muse (and editor).

Publication History

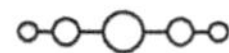

The following stories first appeared in:

"An Adventure in Art Appreciation" – *Defiant Scribe*

"Always on the Run" – *Potato Soup Journal*

"Christmas Ghosts" – *Defiant Scribe*

"Daddy Long Legs" – *Defiant Scribe*

"The Dollhouse" – *365 Tomorrows*

"The Holding Area" – *Aethlon: The Journal of Sport Literature*

"It's the Water" – *Defiant Scribe*

"Marikina" – *Short Edition*

"One of These Days" – *Defiant Scribe*

"Orientation" – *365 Tomorrows*

"Romance, Shromance" – *Defiant Scribe*

"Skunk" (appeared as "Night in the City") – *101 Words*

"Still or Sparkling" – *Dream Noir*

"Transformation" – *365 Tomorrows*

"Weekend in Tomales Bay" – *Defiant Scribe*

"Shut Up and Write" – Honorable Mention,
Humor Category, 2020 Soul-Making Keats Literary
Competition

About the Author

Photo by Richard Osborn

Greg Roensch is a writer from San Francisco, California. His stories have appeared in *Dream Noir*, *365 Tomorrows*, *Defiant Scribe*, *Potato Soup Journal*, and elsewhere. This is his second collection of short, short stories.

Learn more at www.gregroensch.com.

Before Lunch, There Was Breakfast

If you enjoyed *Lunch with the Alien and Other Short, Short Stories*, be sure to pick up *Breakfast!*

A mysterious woman stumbles into a campground in the dead of the night. Two extra-terrestrials conduct a secret mission in a maternity ward. An arctic guide loses radio contact with his ship. A young island girl dreams of a new life in a foreign land.

In this collection of short, short stories – some just a few paragraphs long – Greg Roensch breathes life into characters from all walks of life and creates whole worlds, many of which exist in the shadowy realm between dream and reality.

Full of chance encounters and missed opportunities, these stories remind us that life is strange, frightening, remarkable … and always surprising.

Available now from your favorite online booksellers.

Learn more at gregroensch.com

www.ingramcontent.com/pod-product-compliance
Lightning Source LLC
Chambersburg PA
CBHW021700110726
47902CB00007B/2011